*A Married Man*

*By Benjamin DeMott*

THE BODY'S CAGE

HELLS & BENEFITS

YOU DON'T SAY

A MARRIED MAN

*Benjamin DeMott*

# A MARRIED MAN

*Harcourt, Brace & World, Inc.*
*New York*

PS
3554
· E468X
M3

*To Lynn Bennion*

*A Married Man*

# 1

At times humor goes, and the sense of proportion. I play hero. I look at others and think: They know nothing. Cowards all, immured in dailiness.

(I admit I don't know much. It simply seems a lot to me, owing to previous ignorance.)

At other times I see a face or say a name aloud. I say the name aloud and sometimes I hear a voice crying out to me, in the cave of my skull, in transport, or else not in transport. Oh God sweetness Gordon oh

Then there is blackishness. Sitting at a red light in my car I notice a breath of depression. What can be done? I wait for the light to change and perceive all at once that I lack truth. I have no truth in me. My life is blank, I am made of nothing. I have respected no belief, taste, word, relation in my life. When I start on this tack I proceed directly to the death theme. My quick sun-honeyed hands, fine black hairs on their backs, my hands that bend round the steering wheel in front of me. What will happen to them? *I have no truth in me.* It's not even in me to know a depth of confusion! If I think of death, I also think how good of me to think this thought. Nothing cuts the self-approval. It's the same at a church wedding or in the john, office or home. Holding myself and looking about me or straight ahead whistling softly I think with satisfaction of my claims as an experienced man. . . . For other people there's not much to the physical life—defecate, pee, headache, the dentist, semimonthly habitual throws, twinges up the ass. A cabdriver once said to me—no, I won't repeat that, too filthy and cynical. Anyway: the point is I can't weep and thoughts of suicide don't enter my mind.

But I want to stop. The habit is a symptom only but it's harmful. It needs to be broken and there's no way. . . .

At night is when I do my thinking. Safely, silently. Walking, or else lying in bed beside my wife, I work out sequences in time, study bits of the past. I concentrate, more or less. I'm by turns sentimental, analytical, objective, proud, embarrassed. . . . I start at a comfortable place, avoiding shames of youth. I go on to the present—a matter of three or four years at most. Or else I go on until I sleep.

Always there is sleep. I'm never hurt, never freed. In my youth I was unhappy, tormented, worse—but rest was no problem. Always there was sleep. I shake myself out of self-satisfaction. I try, yes I do. A hundred times I cry out damn-ingly, soundlessly. I say this and that. I frown, wince. What is the matter with you, man? What are you trying to do? But never am I hurt. These questions—they're all false, they merely rock me to sleep. Beyond the black marks on this page, beyond this voice, this "writer," stands a prisoner. I hear him pleading inside me. Oh how he wants anguish! He isn't anguished, he only wants anguish. Poor buried brute. See me, he whimpers. He begs. Mock me, see me. *Set me free.*

# 2

Nothing more ordinary than the beginnings. I am away from home, naturally. Business trip. A motel. After a period of overinvolvement in the current assignment, I've been experiencing a letdown. As long as we were in New York it was tolerable. I liked being away from the home office and walking to work in the morning. Also I liked seeing the high-priced men and women polished and primped and avaricious—impressing each other and stealing each other's space. . . . Everyone in my office tends to take up a positive, go-ahead selflessness that's oppressive.

But we couldn't stay in New York once in production. (My firm makes science strips and features.) The nights were bad. Supper in a hotel dining room, work afterward in the unit producer's room, downstairs to the bar and Irish whiskey and stories about The Stars. (There were contract people on this series, commercials, rented tape truck and so forth.) I remember one or two girls. A chubby jolly Jewish lass clomping about in rubber boots. Also a researcher people called by her last name. She came to my hotel with a script once and instead of leaving it at the desk rode up in the elevator and knocked at my door. Thin and tiny, like a waif in a French picture. I also remember the packing and unpacking and the sameness of the food and drink—room-service orange juice, New York cuts, double martinis. . . .

We were in Washington for a while and in Philadelphia and Boston and then there was a break. Then we were in Minnesota and back to Chicago and again out to Wisconsin. They were one and the same place.

The last night of the first midwest trip we ate in a hotel by a lake. The producer was talking and I turned away and the girl beside me said what did I think when I saw myself in the tape truck, the monitors. I blushed for some reason. It was interesting, I said—how you look to others, how you look to yourself, etc. I was not telling the truth. It was not interesting to me. It was absorbing. I loved my face in the monitors, the texture of my skin. I lost myself staring at my image. "The identity bit?" she said. No, I said, it was the selectivity that interested me. "Oh," she said, "the appearance-reality bit." I shook my head and began rambling. I didn't want to stop talking. The idea I thought I was getting at was difficult, I explained, not clear even to me. I frowned as though I saw the idea hanging in the air in front of me. I was about to lie and did not know what lie it would be. Her waiting-watching expression was humorous and intelligent, very young. The point was, I said, if you see yourself as others see you at a moment you're perfectly clear what they ought to be seeing—because you yourself remember exactly what you felt and thought and were at that moment—well then—

"Jean, honey," said a writer who was listening to us. "Who do you have to fuck to get off this show?"

"Whom," Jean corrected him.

I said that what I was talking about was all in Sartre some place.

"The looker-looked-at bit?" Jean said. "Philosophy 23?"

"That's it," the writer said. "Sartre the writre."

Jean told him to shush.

"You look lovely," the director said to me, sincerely drunk. "You're a very sweet person. I mean that, Doctor. It comes across. They could have sent anybody, Einstein, Dr. Spock—"

"He's neat," the writer said. He was in a bad humor about a script. "Interested in what the young chemists say. Not faking it."

I said, speaking in the right tone, that I was somebody you could trust.

Laughter brimmed in Jean's face.

"Doctor Flint," the director said. His name was Freddie. "Doctor, you promised." He shook his finger loosely at me and forgot what I promised.

The producer ordered more drinks. As the waiter left,

8

Freddie slid off the chair to the floor and sat there smiling with his eyes closed.

"—a very sweet person," Freddie said to everyone, "don't let them say you're not. I mean it. A *very* sweet person."

# 3

"I'm going swimming," Jean said, back at the motel. The others were putting Freddie to bed. It was warm and there was a huge low moon, close and yellow. I changed into my trunks quickly. The mirror stared at my naked chest—I pawed through my bag for a sweater. Seemingly, people were on the bed, talking about me. I cleared the bath towels from the rack and took a blanket and ran.

The pool was closed, doors locked. The water lapped neatly in the breeze, gorgeous blue in the floodlights. A notice said no swimming after sunset.

Jean shrugged. She had errands at the office.

She was barefoot, carrying her towel, cigarettes. We returned through the carpeted corridor. I left her at the street map on the wall and went into the office, pretending I wanted to find somebody about the pool. The office was empty. She was standing in front of the street map when I came out. She hadn't been studying it all this time. I knew this from the set of her mouth and eyes. She was overintent. "Jefferson Turnpike blah-blah-blah," she said. She told me the name of the street she wanted. We were picking up two guests the next morning, a rescheduled interview. She followed a road with her finger, and air stirred on my skin. Perfume rose from her shoulders. It was very still in the corridor, thin heating sounds muffled in the carpeting. I felt the space around her shaped by her breathing and small movements. She was tall and fair. The thought in my head was of the way touching the white cloth of her bathing suit would instantly dry off my palms.

It was my eye that found the street.

"Wowser," Jean said, writing on a pad in her hand. "Quick and clever *and* neat and clean."

We went down the hall not speaking. I was irritated at my hesitations. I thought: Stand at her door and talk a minute and ask her to have a drink. Strongly and calmly. Not too strongly.

I stopped at her door. I did not say I was sorry about the swim. I did not say we would swim another time. I moistened my lips to speak and said good night, as she hunted for her key. She answered me smiling, gave a small salute with her hand and went into her room.

# 4

The second break came—I'm moving straight along, making no more of anything than I made then—the second break came and I sat in my cubicle reading journals and running protection tapes after my section left for the day. It happened as I might have expected. Sitting alone in the dark watching lab tricks I felt her face smiling with me in the darkness. Not from the screen, simply in the darkness with me. I flicked the light button and began scribbling comments, berating the production side in approved home-office cut-and-slash style. . . .

I played tennis and spent a morning playing gardener—clipping hedges and shrubs while my wife weeded. My wife is a serious gardener. When the office was dull I went to my windows and looked out at the lawn and the highway. I thought about what might be happening at home and felt decent and loving. Coming into the kitchen in the evening I caught my wife from behind and kissed her neck and she looked round at me—surprise, pleasure, feigned impatience. My restlessness—this is the common word and I accept it—my restlessness went away. I talked playfully in the tone that reminds me of domestic movies I saw as a boy, Lewis Stone, etc. The voice also owes something to a memory of my father teasing my mother. I said how hard it must be to live without me for a week, time must pass slowly, how entertaining to have me home. People on the project sympathized with her in her deprivation, I said. While I was speaking, no thought of another face, no distraction, touched my mind. I felt kindly. Generous. I saw myself in the glass, straightforward features, expressive mouth. Everything would go on, after all, even if I said nothing. My wife would go on with dinner and the boys and the dog would come in, the house would stand, the lawn would grow and be mowed and swept and edged, if I never spoke again, if I never said another teasing word. But I was magnanimous. I said things. Kissing my wife's neck was largesse too—no different from the joking. Double proof of fidelity. "What's got into you!" Perfect trust and ease. Or when one of the boys whistled at us. Children like to see Mother and Dad making out. I was building their security. I was good.

Toward the end of the break the boys and I went off one morning canoeing, first making sandwiches in the kitchen and then driving to the river and parking and packing down to the water. The pollution stink was terrific. But the sun was enormous and the shores were green and fresh. Both my boys are blond—different from me. They begin bleaching out in May and their skin turns gold. They are well-shaped lads—straight limbs, long muscles, faces that will grow strong or else turn indeterminate, sensitive, pleasant, nothing for long. I am vain of their golden skin and their gold-blond hair. I look at them and think. In the boat I saw them as beautiful, their beauty deriving from my wife and me. We were mixed in their features, good points coming through intact. Once, curving around an island, curving so softly and perfectly through the water it might have been air, sliding downhill, the younger lad leaning back half-asleep under his ragged boater, arms on the gunwales, the older stroking nicely in the bow—once I wanted literally to touch them. I wanted to move forward and stroke their rich lean golden skin! I shook my head at myself. It was love, was it not? I loved their very names. I was brooding about this—was it love or incipient middle-age queerness?—when the younger lad put his arm over the side, trailing a hand in the water. I yelled at him, repelled. It shook my mood, seeing the boy's hand in the stinking water. Uncycled waste. He looked around at me puzzled. I waved dismissingly, taking up the stroke.

We came home thirsty and arm-sore, faces hot. I made drinks, liking my provisioning self as I moved bottles and glasses about. "—the kind of man who does what has to be done." Paddle. Negotiate. Mix. We sat in the garden in the long evening until the sun dropped out of the elms and the air dampened. The lights of the shopping center on the highway began on-and-off flaring behind the trees. We ate in sweaters on the terrace with the blackness peeping everywhere. The candle flames still. I thought: I think I am content. Lilac thickened in the air. I remembered, comfortably, something the doctor said to me a year or so before. My wife was recovering from an illness. The doctor said in answer to my question that ideas of death were melodramatic. Yet it made sense, if there were things you wanted to do, not to postpone them. He gave me a glance. Shouldn't live as though you have forever, he said. Nobody should. It was pleasing in some way to think that—but then what would you do? I thought of the joke about the man who said to his wife: If one of us dies before the other, I think I'll go to Paris to live. Freud speaks of this joke. At moments like the one in the garden it was plain enough—was it plain enough?—that ours were simple desires. We only wanted to sit with a drink waiting for the begonias, counting the recognizable bird songs. *Rogue Male* was the book that was being read aloud. I read by candlelight after supper and lucked into a thrilling bit. The boys were attentive. Later that night I thought of calling a Berkeley friend on the chance of finding a house to rent. A vacation *en famille*. A surprise. My friend liked fixing things for people. The boys had never been west. They and their mother could have a car, see what they wanted. I could look in during breaks. . . .

At noontime the next day I shut my study doors at home

and, feeling expansive, I called California and explained what I wanted. As I was explaining, my mind changed. I no longer wanted them with me. You're in luck, my friend said. He was enthusiastic. His neighbor had just been talking about subletting for a month, not too far up the hill, five bedrooms, a pool. . . . There was important stuff for us to talk about, yes yes, lots of laughs, absolutely, we had to come. I felt myself frowning at the man's good humor and enthusiasm and heard myself back away—plans not set, might fall through. . . . I sat on for a moment after hanging up, listening to the voices in the kitchen. There was no particular thought in my head. I was simply waiting. I remember I came in to them smiling in father style, thinking: Change again, why not? The boys would prance around the kitchen table when they knew. They would throw gloves at the ceiling and need to be shouted at. I sat down with them and began talking. A family excursion. A few weeks or a month. California. I was on the phone finding us a house—a nice place or even a not-so-nice place. My face felt rueful, a life of its own. What was the trouble? It wasn't my personal mind that spoke. The difficulty, I explained, was that we had only a month and people wouldn't rent for this short a time. There was one place— perfect, spacious, nice pool. . . . But no, nothing available for our short time.

The boys were bored after the first minute, unimpressed. I turned cold. They were spoiled, took too much for granted. It hadn't occurred to them that I needn't have bothered to think of them at all. There was no law requiring me to. When I spoke my manner was stern, hurt. All right, no reason why they should care one way or the other. As long as they understood that while I was away they had a special obligation not to harass their mother. I went on in a down-pressing voice, spelling out the behavior expected while I was gone. I paused from time to time, waiting for my wife to nod in support of what I said. I felt clearheaded and dutiful. *Sound.* Not once, surprisingly, did the faraway consciousness—faraway but still alert and fascinated—not once did the faraway consciousness of my falsity embarrass me or lighten my voice or soften the warning force I bent on them with my eyes.

# 5

So California. I traveled by myself and the last leg ran backward, east from the coast a half hour toward the mountains—a strange landscape, brown earth heaped in piles, small brown hills, sudden square green islands. The light faded quickly behind us. . . . The pilot stayed close to the ground. He was a talkative man who went on about you picture people and gave me a flying lesson. Small planes make me feel coextensive, made of wings and glass, throbbings and air. My forehead opens, the roof of my skull is glass, sky, clouds—I'm childlike, free, open to the heavens, a bare, blown bird. You picture people, the pilot said, you picture people ought to buy you a plane, the way you like it so much. I concentrated on the compass, feeling my body fade off from the bearing again. The heat thrummed, I let my arms go limp without loosening my grip on the wheel. "That auburn-haired brunette girl," he went on. "Yes," I said. "She couldn't get enough of it, swear to God. She wanted to set it right down by herself without aye yes or no. Some gal." Leaning forward to catch the light on the compass, I saw Jean in my place. I imagined her hands, long pale fingers holding the wheel lightly, her face bemused but serious as she aimed at the line of hills ahead. . . . The intrusion in her day, a picture of her taken without her knowledge, was like money found in the street. My arms felt stronger after a minute, and only when we were over the strip and the pilot said in his drawl that he would take her down for form's sake did I give up the sweet dancing craft in my hands.

We were traveling and shooting, collecting beauty shots. The balance of nature. I was dispensable. I looked unsuccessfully for Jean and then worked at my typewriter for an hour. Later I walked to the pool and watched the swimmers. The park was crowded, thousands of families, baton twirlers, blubber midriffs in shorts. A thin dust rose from the tramped valley floor and hung in the sunlight between the trees. The crew was in the park restaurant bar when I found them—but not Jean. She and Freddie were missing. I stayed with the crew at the bar, drinking and listening.

At supper and later people worked at being tight and hilarious. The lighting man took over a recreation hall. The assistant director, Freddie's helper, played the piano and the cue-card girl and the floor manager danced and the producer sang. In his youth the producer had quit college to join a road-company chorus. Watching him perform I had a glimpse of how he looked to himself, his inner life—how he believed in the beauty of his open mouth, his teeth, his glistening eyes. His voice—a "cascade of song." I believed I couldn't be wrong about any of this, but it did not interest me, didn't matter. The writer who was scratchy the night at the lake sat with some others telling stories about The Stars to the producer's wife. I listened, enjoying my separateness. It was late when Jean came in. She was with Freddie. They began dancing. I tried not to let it be seen how I watched them. I knew from her movements Jean was dancing in a manner detached and amused, as though her partner wasn't a person. They were doing imitations of ballroom champions. The music changed to Cuban, and Freddie's worn good looks reorganized into professional spik arrogance. He was amusing. Drunk, he nevertheless missed no steps. I felt envy growing in me as I watched, and I was ashamed. My palms were wet. I was sweaty and tense inside my clothes. They came very close to me and their muscled force moved the air around my face. My forehead was wet and I ached with something.

The park police came and ended it. People picked themselves up slowly and hung about outside. The lighting man stood on the curb telling a dialect story, and I saw Jean listening. I knew at that instant exactly how I wanted her to be listening. Not with distaste. Hoping the story would be amusing enough to make coarseness worthwhile. Knowing, as she hoped, that seldom did this happen. Was she aware I was standing near her, waiting and listening?

Someone shouted from the lodge across the street. Children trying to sleep, shut up. I said good night abruptly, illustrating responsible behavior. The producer came by my room a minute later and gave me a bottle. "I heard you typing before," he said and winked. "I know you intellectuals."

My window looked out into a bank of pines. Overhead a great waterfall came breathing down the mountainside. I felt nagged, unfinished. I sat at the typewriter and wrote to my wife. The subject was responsibility, the refusal to accept. I spoke judgingly of the producer and his wife. I explained that they had a young child yet were not troubled to have left him behind in Manhattan, or to find themselves shouted at like teen-agers late at night, thousands of miles from the fruit of their union. . . . My writing was even heavier than this, and I was not ashamed of it. When I stopped typing I heard insects bumping and buzzing at the screens in the night dampness that came into the room and touched my skin. Cold breath. The falls made a long washing sound. Drops of perspiration slid down my bare sides. I leaned back imagining the falls exploding high up, clouds of glory, mist folding in the moonlight, sinewy, dancelike. I imagined the park before it was a park, before human exploitation, flatness, pointlessness. . . . I reread what I had written and shook my head at the priggishness but decided my wife would find these sentiments reassuring. I went into the bathroom and studied myself in the mirror. There was no vanity in this. I went looking for confirmation. For a time, thinking of nobody, I dozed on my pillow in peace.

# 6

The telephone rang.

"While you're up get me my Grant's," Jean said. "Where is it? I've got a headache."

I didn't speak and she said, "I know, I'm interrupting the management blah-blah-blah. Your light's on. Bert said you needed a bottle so I was nice. I'll come get it."

She hung up. I looked at my watch. It was 1:30. At the window it was too black to see the falls. I was straightening the bathroom when she knocked. She was wearing white pants and a striped top. There were freckles at her collarbone. She stood with her feet crossed in a pretty pawky way. In the doorway I asked her to have a drink and told her I hadn't opened the bottle.

I went down the hall to the ice bin with glasses and

filled them without thinking. When I came back she was sitting at the desk reading the production daily I finished that afternoon.

"Do you mind, she said red-handedly," Jean said.

I put her drink down on the desk without smiling. When she finished reading she turned the chair around and leaned her chin on the top of it looking at me.

"I looked for you this afternoon," I said. I sat on the couch.

"This road bit is awful, everybody jammed together. I never see a soul from the office in New York. Absolute perfect separation. I love it. People try and I just say, Hop off."

"Proud Maisie."

"I do like Freddie Kilham," she said, frowning. "He's a fundamentally nice person. Even drunk."

"Yes?"

"You know he's a fairy, of course."

I nodded.

"Marty Kliegl said that to Bert once and Bert almost killed him. Bert hates knowing things. He's afraid he'll lose his innocence."

She went on talking "maturely" about homosexuality and about not wanting to know the truth. I decided she was about twenty-six. I felt myself being shrewdly patient and unimportunate in lechery. We talked about jobs. Her last job had been in Washington. I asked her about college and her family, her father's work and did she have sisters and brothers. I listened carefully as she spoke, hearing at moments something true and full, not trivial, in her voice. But the next second I could not remember what she had said, and twice she chuckled and told me she had just *told* me. I was able to remember only that she was the youngest child. Each time I freshened the drinks I told her to get out of the straight chair, we had a long drive tomorrow and she ought to relax. She and Freddie and I were to drive one of the rented cars to a fairly distant drop in the morning. The third time I went for ice I saw a white strip against the darkness at the top of the mountain. For a second I was puzzled.

"Dawn," I said as I came back into the room.

"Regrets." She had moved from the chair to the couch. She was sitting with her knees beneath her chin, looking straight ahead. I sat on the couch with her.

"I've been thinking for an hour the next minute I'd kiss you. That's why I didn't listen."

"I hoped it was that."

I kissed her. Her tongue was small and wild. She leaned back with her eyes closed, lips apart. Deliberately, patiently, I undid her clothes. She watched my hands gravely and kissed them when they were near her face. Her nipples, straight and alive, sent a delicate fear through me at the touch, as though it might be dangerous for my hands to touch her.

"I know what," she said. Her lips were light and cool, tulipy against my mouth as she spoke. I felt the fiery smell of tobacco smoke down through the center of her like a root of fury. "You put nasty drugs in the scotch."

"Everything," I said. I kissed her neck, her shoulders, her

24

throat, her hair. I was still helping her with her clothes.

"Doctor, we love what you're doing but—"

I had not stopped murmuring to her, and she said, "Oh *God*—" and I kissed her again, fearful of her excitement and elevated by it, as though everything she was and felt and said were my invention. It seemed to me I had barely touched her when, with a childlike sound, pitiably unprotected, she shuddered sweetly through herself into me and we met.

# 7

That morning, our awakening and parting, I focused intently on details—money for the maid, lock typewriter, stamps, collect toilet articles, the breakfast cart out in the hall. . . . As I packed I went over the hours before and after dawn and chided myself for insufficient detachment at breakfast—instead of sitting calmly, accepting Jean's presence and the fact of the breakfast we ordered (in the wilderness there is room service), I talked oversolicitously. . . .

At one point, I realized, Jean smiled at me as at a child.

I reminded myself as I packed to be thorough about packing and if I did forget something, not to go back for it.

Suddenly there was excitement racing in the room like a bird fluttering wildly against glass. I *saw* Jean turning toward me to speak. The picture went off and left a stillness —a rustling of the air followed by nothingness followed by absolute stillness. I'd never been surprised and embarrassed in this way before. Standing in the room by myself I saw the softness and pliancy of near-sleep in her skin and eyes, her head bent forward, her cheek resting on her knees. I stood straight, trying to remember. Inside me I felt a queer inexpressible lightness and curiosity.

Easiness was the right thing, I reminded myself. Calm, nothing overvoluble, overexpressive. I stood in the room rubbing my shaven cheeks and trying to take fresh hold of my thoughts.

I wasn't getting on with packing. Sleepy and inefficient —my hands only shuffled clothes from one bag to the other, irresolute. Half my mind was manipulating, calculating. Avoid any hint of possessiveness, I thought. I looked around the room and saw wrinkles on the couch cover, Jean's coffee cup, cigarettes in the tray. . . . I straightened everything hastily, mocking myself but not stopping, and sat my bags neatly against each other and the typewriter.

And then again as I glanced at the window I felt quickness and softness coming together out of the air into a presence. I stared at the place and just at that moment remembered myself listening somewhere some time to a forgotten person tell about a kindly ghost that appeared—where? The hallway of a summer house? Who was it? The small faint Jean-image in my head, this dozing promiscuous sexandthesinglegirlchild—it was one minute out of how many? How many exactly? One-thirty when she called . . . I stood in the middle of the room looking at my watch, adding and subtracting hours, calculating as though there were no urgent question but this in the world.

Up the path people were in the way when I came out with my bags. A man bending over tieing a shoelace for a boy. The man's wife, wearing Bermuda shorts and carrying a stuffed shoulder bag and a camera. Coming toward them I felt safe, returned. Relief, a surge of fellow-feeling. The same the world over, mothers, fathers, central parental cares, parental kindness, *Gemütlichkeit* . . . The couple was an oasis. But I looked coldly over their heads as I came near, hurrying to the car, and passed them unbreathingly, as though they were a smell.

# 8

I drove, and we were away from the park quickly, top down in the brilliant sun. Nobody talked. Freddie was unshaven. After a time we saw signs for the big trees reservation, and Freddie and Jean spoke at once. The place was out of our way. I turned off and drove into the woods.

We were in a deep stillness, bronze-shadowed. Deer sprang through columns of sunlight. Jean pointed without speaking. Close by, a doe stared, alive to the tremblings of its own breath. At the sight of the great trees I stopped, wordless. I remember thinking: No preface. All at once the trees—a massive brown thereness waiting in the earth. The stillness of the brown light made us speak confinedly, close to ourselves, as though warding off a spell. Freddie got out to take a picture. I didn't look at him or at Jean. In my mind I kept touching an intuition of our insignificance, our not-mattering, the pretentiousness of seeing this and that as good or bad.

We stayed awhile, speaking out loud about the light, the quiet, the way shadows fell, the enormity of the trees. I knew we were talking about something that could not be seen. It was beyond sensation. At one moment I was moved so powerfully to say untrivial words, something true, that the longing made my jaws move involuntarily.

On the sunny highway again Freddie changed our mood. He hummed tunes from the night before. English somewhere once, he had a neat, bright, Fred Astaireish voice— too young and too old for him. I looked inside him and saw the wrongness of condescending to him. Why should he care for Rigor, Discipline, what have you. (I had again been hard on the production people in my daily.) He wasn't a child to be "educated," lived amid realities of his own, was too old to be cajoling contract crews, scrambling on hillsides in his ripped denim shorts setting up "interesting shots." Why worry about his waist, why entertain the producer, Bert, why be a charming drunk and tactful homosexual? They were singing cocktail piano clichés together, Freddie and Jean, if we'd thought a bit of the end of it—I'd even face wedlock—like a sip of sparkling burgundy brew . . . I nodded to myself, grasping something new and at the same time feeling something loosen within me. They did the songs well, missing few words or notes. Jean's voice was direct, pure, unself-conscious. "Ducks, guess what," Freddie broke off singing, "guess what, we've missed the plane." Then he said, "Oh damn the bastards, there's always another."

We gave up the car in the drop city, and the place burned in our shoe bottoms as we waited for a taxi. What are we? I thought, standing thousands of miles from my regularities. Friends, charming friends? Having shared a moment of natural piety among the trees, God's sentinels, etc., we now become comfy old shoes as in a thirties flick, Katharine and Cary and Edward Everett inspiring love in waiters, postmen, corner cops, making people turn to admire their pretty animation? Freddie teased the cabdriver when he came, joking about the climate of the place, its advantages. Sun turns off at midnight, the driver explained, only it doesn't do any good because, you see these buildings, they're regular gray-ut big heaters at night and they go awhomping and whomping the heat out in waves until each time you pass them you're starting to lose a pound or two in pure worry and just as soon's they start losing some heat, just soon's— "I love your little old town," Freddie said to the man when we got out. "That's right kind, Mister," the driver said. "You're not so bad yourself."

It was not different on the plane—or at the motel when we were there. Freddie went ahead of us, and Jean sat across the aisle from him. Jean said wasn't she nice to save me the window. "Please take it," I said. These were the first words I had spoken only to her since we kissed "gaily" at the door after breakfast and she went off to pack. She smiled and shook her head. The stewardess came with iced tea, and when we finished it, Jean opened her bag and took out a pretty blue flask. She poured scotch into my cup and then into Freddie's. The stewardess looked mock-crossly at us, grinning a noncompany grin. I was lighter in my physical self. I knew we were different from the others on the plane, fresher in energy, less cloddish.

It was the same at the Hollywood motel, sitting and talking, eating together, having the place explained to us. The small lobby was full of bundles of laundry and cleaning. The clerk said hello in friendly Western and said if we ate outside would we please remind Red to charge us something, Red forgot to make out checks for pool lunches and it was a nuisance. Jean said, Homey. Freddie left to meet his agent. The desk man led us down the hall and unlocked Jean's place for her and motioned me to follow and I went on without reminding Jean to say when she was ready. I grimaced at this but only for a second. What did it matter? Everything was delicious, opportune. Excitement took me when I was alone again. The place was a two-story pentagonal housekeeping motel hollowed out with Kodachrome palm trees and pool. My apartment—a kitchen, with barstools, in the living room, a bedroom, a terrace with a view of a four-bay gas station and a Christian Science church . . . Unpacking I noticed a musty chlorine stink in the room, sogginess in the carpet. People dripped down the hall from the pool, not caring? The chair on the terrace was rusted. But it didn't matter, stupid to notice. The place was cosy and private, snug. . . . I showered and dressed and called Jean, studying myself in the mirror as I spoke to her. I spoke teasingly, watching myself. Would she think of eating with me, etc.—detached, sensible, "humorous." My tone said, No, I would not presume, no mean vulgarity, no sense of "entitlement."

In the lobby, going off to dinner, we met the crew. They wanted to joke with Jean. Somebody explained that the motel was full of second bananas. I frowned at Jean's listening eyes. How could she be interested? Full of second bananas from Pat O'Brien movies, crazy, said Kliegl the unit producer. If you looked you saw faces you couldn't place, kid-brother types, desk sergeants, hoods from the Edouardo Cianelli mob. Crazy. I laughed with the others. Why would we want to be alone? Why not forget dinner and stand here and talk . . . I felt questioning eyes on me. The others were wondering about us? Something going on there? Vanity rose in me. I didn't mind waiting longer.

Outside on the street the air was sweet and warm but bit the eyes. We ate in a restaurant with the local view—gas stations, cars, lighted houses, cars. I was lordly about the hors d'oeuvre cart and about decanting the wine. We hardly talked during the meal, though the food was ordinary. Now and then I felt a sudden connectedness of thought and feeling between us and my breath left me. Jean said we were eating like savages. She told a story about clever ways she knew of expensing luxo bottles and meals. Once we paused, suspended in the air. Amusedly I grew conscious of our jaws masticating more slowly. Chewing more and more slowly for fear chewing made each in the other's gaze less handsome. I felt no fear, only a cautious canny elation—a familiar confidence about the sequel, a wish merely to smile.

Then we were back in Jean's living room.

"You were so nice," Jean said. "I liked you all day."

"Good," I said. "I like your flask."

"Bergdorf. If you don't watch out Freddie'll fall in love with you."

"He tried me, didn't I say?"

Jean looked at me hard and I told how it happened. I was standing up in a bar, Milwaukee, I thought, getting money out, and Freddie made a pass at me.

She seemed skeptical, so I explained.

"They bump into you and touch you here and here. Big accident. There's a technical name for it. They give you a smile."

"It sounds lovely."

"It's not. Don't be cute."

"People keep bumping into you and wanting to make love so naturally it gets very boring."

I looked at her, then let out my breath as though I felt too much to speak.

She resumed opening her letters, moving slightly away. I rubbed my cheeks and asked about her mail. I was annoyed at these childish affected withdrawals, pauses. Jean made her comic-pedantic sound and sat very straight.

"The father sends my check, numero one." She held up an envelope. "Lovely lovely check. Lovely lovely Old Brahmin Trust." She held up something else. "Numero two, the mother. The mother says she's worried."

"Why aren't you married?"

"You sound like the mother, actually."

"Why not answer?"

"I almost got married. His name was Charles." She rolled her eyes. "Ziss vuss beeg, Charles und Jean."

"When? Please don't be cute."

"Washington. 'It wasn't right,' quotation."

"Did you sleep with him? I'm sorry—"

"Not always, she said shyly. I mean not all the time, of course." She dropped her eyes. "Once," she said. " 'We didn't fit down there,' quotation."

Neither of us spoke for a minute. She lifted the mail from her lap in two hands and held it up looking at it as though deciding whether to see it as an offering or a mess. I was trembling. The column of air down through the center of me—I was becoming this column. I saw suppressed laughter in her eyes, and in the lamplight her hair—it was auburn hair and she wore it long—was extremely beautiful. I wanted to shout in it, I wanted it over my face like a sweet cover. Rich and soft. My muscles lifted my hands with a force and will of their own.

"I thought I wouldn't go home tonight," I said. "I mean, back to my barstools."

"Really."

"I was going to stay here. And then later I could go home."

"Is that it," she said. She clasped her lower lip with her upper, innocence shocked. "It's rather confident, isn't it."

"No," I said into her hair. My head moved with a ferocity not mine, and at once we were bound to each other again, harsh urgent tongues and arms and hands.

# 9

Now it was that I began to talk, turning myself into a talking machine. It was an attempt at magic. Was it not possible, I said, that I might be incapable of making love? I said, How was it we didn't know any better than to forget that possibility? Having traveled a distance by car and air, having enjoyed Freddie and having parted with him, having found our new home and settled in it and unpacked, having had no rest the night before, having eaten and having read her mail, we were falling asleep, I said, yet acting as though we knew no better than to believe I could make love again. Didn't she believe in weariness? Didn't she know any of the relevant jokes? I said I was, after all, decrepit, collapsed. I'd seen signs of decay of the body in myself since age twenty-eight. There was a line in my derrière, a symbol of fallenness. Had she not read in magazines that as an Older Man I had to be treated with consideration? Medically considered, best for us not to try? . . . I waited for her naked as she bathed and then lay beside her unstirring for a time. Her body was cool, long-limbed. My fingers moved the length of her into sweet sliding smoothness that stopped my breath. Touching her lightly with one finger, I said this was extravagance on her part, was it not? I had asked her to take facts and probabilities into account. "Isn't it talkative and articulate and all," she said. "You could do more here, Older Man, she said lubriciously," Jean said, placing my other hand, "it's an omission." I thought again sadly: One among many, comparative sex. We lay together and she took me into her hand and we kissed. There was a heaviness inside me that mere love-making could not touch, and I used words to lighten it, hide it, drive it off. "Think of it," I said out loud. "I hate talking people," she told me against my lips. "Behave." "Think of it," I said again. "Think of arrangements being what they are," and gently I took her on top of me, "think of its being there and these desiccated types talking—it's so *men*tal." "Very," she said. *"Doc*tor," she said, taking her breath in quickly as I entered her. Her chin trembled, her face came together in exquisite nonpain. "But if we go on as we are—" I said. "Assume that," she said, smiling into nowhere beatifically, "assume going on." "And nothing happens. I mean nothing at all, nothing—I'm wrecked, withered, staled—old diddler. So," I went on. I wanted my body and my voice to be one consistency, a unity. "So," I said, "if I'm talking, if I talk talk talk, then nobody has to be ashamed. I won't have let you go so far toward—" "Oh darling you can't—" "Jean?" "You can't be ashamed. You're so beautiful, you—Oh sweetness—" Her face was thrown back, contorted. I was afraid again of the deepened fury of feeling in it but iron-proud, impersonally iron-proud. I told her she was not in control, as though impatient with her. "Oh I'm not, I'm not, I'm—am I?" Then breathless she bent forward stopping me. "Darling don't—" "Jean—" "If you do that I can't wait—" Then it was as it is. We were mounting rapidly and there was a billowing of seas beneath us, the first long sustained unanxious love-making of strangers, smooth and mountainous, continuous in unreversible force. "Oh my God, am I—" Jean's teeth were together, eyes tight closed. She quaked, seized me, stopping me again, and everything dropped away, I rose higher, cresting, laving her now not hasty as before but slow, wresting, climbing, thrusting, and she cried out, her fingers tore at me, I was perfectly even, I saw her wild hair and eyes and her mouth, her eyes gazing off at something measureless and a scream tore itself out of me early, I rose straight up as though sucked into the center of her motion and being and screaming together we came.

We fell upon each other like beaten swimmers on a lucky strand, bewildered, not trusting the end. I heard wonderingly in my memory the sound that had come out of me and did not believe in it. It could not have been my voice. For an instant we were both intensely within each other, aware we were totally unprotected. I was still inside her but we looked at each other shyly at that moment, breathless, full of trusting shame.

If I moved, her eyes would open. I knew this for an hour before I spoke. I lay motionless, finding my way back. I studied her sleep, her cool skin, by the light of the street lamp. I said her name and she awakened unstirringly. "Jean," I said again, feeling the breath of my speaking come back to my face from her skin. The cool length of her body turning into me choked the air inside me. "Would it be nice to talk?"

# 10

Often she woke me while it was still dark and we were lying together. The air would be warm, a closeness in the room, her scent and mine mingling in lassitude and cigarette smoke. How did she wake me, what did she do? Did she move close to me whispering, her lips touching my cheeks? Always when I opened my eyes her eyes were gazing at me and she smiled and did not move. I smothered the cry within me, a leaping shout at the incredible immeasurable matchless— A heightening of the moment came from the silence and from the thin dim light and from our not yet having spoken, and I did not break it. With slow dreamlike movements I drew myself to my knees, aware of the sun behind the shade. I seemed not to look into her eyes and kissed her breasts only lightly going down. I breathed into her hair, feeling the warmth of my breath in the feathery fierce tangle. And here I hovered, merely breathing, touching her so lightly with my lips and tongue. . . . I was in a play, an actor caught in the mystery I meant to create, religiously patient, touching, kissing. She said my name, her voice hung between points. It asked me to listen and understand she was awake, humorous, caught in no trance. . . . But if you are, if you are, if you mean . . . Lifting her I hold her a surveying minute, and she trembles, closes her eyes kissing the air, her lips are apart, her nipples taut, and I press her close, moving her away, moving her into me as the shade moves slightly with the breeze and a sudden brightness stripes us both with gold. I thrust and thrust, and she draws in her breath almost hoarsely and begins slowly to know, to fathom the smooth dartings and fierce entrances, to know the love of my tongue and lips cannot end. The day disappears: there is only her movement, her movement with mine, her marvelously excited darting aliveness everywhere against me—

Her eyes are absolutely still, a puzzle disappearing in languor, as they look at me. I move away from her slowly and come then to kiss her mouth. "Nobody—" she begins. "How you must want me to give me such—" I stop her mouth again and lie beside her wordless. She sleeps, her fingers touching my lips. . . . After moments, an hour, a fragment, excitement wakes us again. As though absently I touch her lightly with my fingers, playfully. She doesn't quiver and she is beautifully wet. She turns toward me and covers my hand between her thighs and, her eyes still closed, moves my hand with hers. As I enter her she whispers in my mouth, wild unheard words. . . . I am steel, invulnerable, cannot be caught. I sing in her ear of her taste and her wildness. She rocks and is shaken and crashes upon me almost instantly and I lie back holding her, not sensing, waiting, asking nothing, waiting. In time we begin again. We lie upon each other, laughing, calling ourselves specimens, calling ourselves ridiculous, we kiss each other off, hold each other back, we are harsh, tender, we move from room to room, we stand, we sit. . . . Soaked from the bath we are slippery brute bodies out of the cool pond onto the hot sand and we fuck roughly wildly tearing at each other shouting in the blazing lint-spinning sun-poured light over the bed.

Our skin glows in the soft air as we walk down the boulevard to a restaurant. We stop and half smile at a sign announcing breakfast served until 5:00 P.M. In a restaurant we order martinis and eggs Benedict. It is mid-afternoon. We go into a theater and watch the titles of a movie and touch each other and walk out desultorily, noticing pictures in the lobby. We look in a bookshop window for ten minutes without speaking. We return to her apartment and undress unhurriedly and lie together. She smokes as we talk. Darkness draws in. We touch each other lazily, perfunctorily, jokingly, menacingly. . . . I hold her away from me and look at her, my hands on her elegant thin beautiful shoulders. . . . Slowly, very slowly, a sense of hours like immovable monuments before us, we begin again to make love.


"I don't know why, sweetness. I don't understand it myself."

"I like a place with a view. I want to share Mary Baker Eddy and CITGO. Come lie with me and tear our pleasure through the reading room and the grease pit—"

She traces my eyelashes. I go on talking, talking. I must not think.

"I make no claim about the bed of course. I don't believe I ever actually—"

"Behave."

"What a miserable mucking place. Look at it. Look at the paper. Look at you—Miss Young New Yorker. Miss Young Thing. Miss Bergdorf, Miss Bonwit, Miss B. I hate a timid mind in a sound body."

"Sweetness, listen to me." She touches my lips with her fingers, moves her fingers across my beard. She separates her words very carefully, like a teacher explaining to first graders. "It's very lovely of you to want me to come to your apartment and I know exactly why you want it and what you feel and it's very sweet and some time I'm going to come, I think. But not yet, please? Can't I wait just a little?"

"Look at it." I point at the walls. I want to be absurd, infantile, impossible. "Wens and Rorschachs. Look at it. Barf."

She slides down between my legs. She begins kissing me.

"Maisie—"

My breath is gone. She presses me backward with one hand.

"It's my house and I can do what I want. Be still."

"It's—"

I lie back with my head on the pillow. I reach out and touch her hair as it falls forward on my stomach.

"Jesus Lord." My voice vanishes inside me as she takes me very deeply between her lips. "Oh my God Jesus Lord my *Je*sus Jean—"

Frowning a little, she looks into a sad middle distance.

"I couldn't have a thing unless it was more than just—"

I kiss her gently and tell her I know this. There is no iron in me, it is as though I am not separately alive, not present. I have melted into her being, I have no structure. Her face is still worried. I smooth her hair, my hand is hers.

"How many times," she speaks without looking at me.

I make a dismissing sound, her words mean nothing. I speak from a deep sleep of self.

"I was honest." Her voice is suddenly fierce. "Hop off, it's not fair for just one to be. I mean, how many besides—" She pushes her face flat into my shoulder. I feel her shaking. "Oh sweetness, I can't, I can't—"

"Never," I hear myself saying. My separate strength returns, protective, hard. "Nobody. Nobody." Crushing memory, grinding it, I believe this myself as I speak.

Returning from supper together we stand beside each other in the lamplight and she studies me in the mirror.

She tells me she has decided I am beautiful, unpainted, weathered, craggy New England ugly-beautiful, hollow cheeks, Abe Lincoln, stony soil, his own style, the rail splitter. All at once she stops giggling. Her voice richens. I hear her school accent in it, and the sound for me is a sound of innocence and memory. I interrupt her again and again as she speaks: "You're canting but your voice is elegant. Canting. Canting." She is explaining that she has spent her days, as long as she can remember, with "attractive people" —they just happen all to be very good-looking, you grow accustomed to it, she knows how awful it sounds, how icky WASPy nice-girl Lindsay worker it sounds, but there it is. . . . And then you go to work and live in the city and you see how many other . . . kinds. And nobody has any character, they don't have lines cut by their eyes, nobody looks hewn and beaten, oh she knows none of this should be "said straight." I smile and tell her she confuses manners, appearances, morals, everything—her mind is a paella, she has no conception of character, she thinks it is jokes and not having credit cards. "I'm not making it into politics, it's experience, that's all," she says. Her manner is nonsilly, adult, competent. Listening I imagine for one instant teaching her, hardening her, feeling pride when her thoughts march. "I'm only saying it's very bad to take that sort of thing for granted—a world of attractive people. It's provincial. This positively infinitesimal minority. I had to learn," she says. "Now I've learned. I don't take anything beautiful for granted."

"I'll tell you what let's do." I sit looking away from her,

frowning. "We both feel like a discussion so let's take off all our clothes very responsibly and neatly and make *motions* and amend and make motions and discuss and discuss and dis*cuss*."

I dive at her and we cling together on the bed, rolling with inexplicable laughter.

Her face is covered with tears as she talks in a rush into my shoulder. "I'm so close, I feel so close, I never came like that, I don't care what you do to it but I'm so close but sweetness you're not *there,* don't you see? Just for one instant and then you're away and I can't touch you so am I here? Am I really here? Am I living inside you? And I want a house here and be in every room here and here and I *am* for one instant and it's so——" She is still weeping, she has no breath when she speaks. "And then you're way away inside yourself into some place and nobody could touch you and it's over."

She leans back, smooths her hair. Paths shine on her cheeks and I kiss them, feeling the moistness on my dry lips. She takes her breath in, speaks in another voice, matter of fact, plain.

"I won't do it again, promise. It just came over me that I'm not you and when I came I thought I was. It's such a shame, such a——"

She throws herself down like a wild child laughingly and covers her head and I see the length of her body quaking under the sheet and am afraid or ashamed, knowing it is not laughter in her but laughter and tears.

There is a pawkish thing in her movement, I discover again and again. She is a quick leggy animal, coltish. This sense comes straight from the posture of her hands and feet. I notice also a tendency toward doggedness, she looks straight ahead when she concentrates, a faint pugilistic quality. It is too affecting—on occasion I have to look away from her. I explain to myself that if lately I've been totally irredeemably ridiculous, it is owing to lack of sleep.

Her father has lost touch with his sons, she says. Also with her sister. The truth may be, she thinks, that her father lives only for her. The small thrusts of sentimentality in what she says bring irony back into my voice. I ask whether she knows she is play-acting. She stops, pauses, laughs. She begins speaking in another voice, still not harsh or unloving, although now she is describing or even discovering her father's weakness, his indulgence of her, his ignorance of her life, fantasies of her innocence—

"Why are you looking at me like that?"

"You can't be truly hard. Even stepping back."

"It's always thinking things, isn't it."

"Not things, no."

She looks at me.

"I only talk a lot because I see you listening and loving to listen and I tell myself, Go on, go on, keep going, he hasn't gone off yet, he's not having his thoughts yet. I'm desperate the second I stop seeing you lost in me." She touches my lips with hers. "Could you possibly understand that, Doctor? It's *very* sick."

Whereas she and the mother are not easy together.

"We don't relax." She lights a cigarette and is pensive. "There're too many people in the world. Too many peops." She seems to be thinking of a particular moment. I want to possess it. Is it simply that her mother was exhausted by three children, nothing left of love for the fourth?

"It's stupid," she says out loud. "It's so ordinary. All gels is scratchy with the Ma. I hate it."

After a moment: "You can't not feel something, though, just because it's a cliché, can you?"

Marvy.
Wowser.
Peops.
Arg.
Troubs.
Blah-blah-blah. Hop off. The Ma. '        ,' she said downrightly. '        ,' she said winningly. '        ,' she said lovingly.

"We were very cute at school," she says. "It's a vicious habit."

She makes breakfast for us one morning and bacon flames up and eggs stick to the pan. She tries to seem un-flapped. I tease her from a cool distance, calling her Maisie, and she tells me again that in her time she has cooked bril-liantly—once at a dinner for eight in her apartment she chose three gourmet dishes, allowed herself hours for pre-paration and produced a sensation. Her guests are still in awe. I suggest they are having her on, has this possibility occurred to her. I tell her there is pomposity even worse than my own in her pretended omnicompetence. I ask her to step outside herself, to look on at her play-acted confidence in her cooking style, to imagine me "observing" that, taking in the dutiful set of her mouth. Imagine me wanting to chuckle at her and not being free to. Having to respect other people's piety. Why is it, I ask, why is it that she can't stand to have her competence challenged? Why must nobody doubt her abilities? What is this fearful need? Has she wondered about it? Shouldn't she wonder? Who on earth, pray, possesses abilities that deserve so much honor? Furthermore, think of the illusions that keep her afloat. Money, for instance. Her claim to be reasonably provident and economical. True, she admits a taste for *objets*. She even admits impulsive extravagances in the picture line now and then. But is it not also true that she wants everything both ways. To be the efficient unwasteful assistant to the producer, general aide, competent, trim, husbanding her one hundred forty or whatever dollars per week, spending wisely and well, shrewd gel, etc. But wants also *not* to be thought of as a working girl, somebody living on her own money. Hints of *snobisme* here? Did she not tell me she spends nine thousand a year, her salary plus half the income of her trust? Isn't she in fact a fantast, a self-deceiver? To call herself independent and so on . . . Charming, oh yes, delicious, amusing, perfection in the morning, Miss Gallery-hopping non-panty-girdled East Sider, Miss Minimini Maisie. *But—*

"Oh I'm *so* sorry," she says gravely. "I just love listening to you because it's so intelligent and all. I'll tell you what," she says as though just struck by a dart of brilliance. "Could you stop for one tiny second and kiss me? And kiss me kissmekissmekissmekissme—"

Opening a drawer in my bureau I see her nightgown folded in a corner. My eyes blur and I fight this. It is a piece of cloth only. I love its presence, defenseless, meek, committed, unjudging. I imagine her folding it carefully, putting it where it is. Her alarm clock in its leather case is on the night table.

"I found something supportive in a drawer today. I picked it up and kissed it." We are in a restaurant. The waiter has gone off with our order.

She is looking about as though interested in the neighboring tables. She comes back to me and smiles.

"Did you like that?" she says. "I thought it might like that."

The waiter has returned with the wine book and he is looking down at us. But our eyes are speaking, our hands have touched, truly we almost do not know the man is there.

# 11

After two weeks the friend who offered me the house I didn't rent drove down and took me to a party. He had threatened this on the telephone beforehand. I went to show Jean I had a life. People came to see me, people wished to see me. . . . I too had a world of shoptalk, shared interests. "An old friend is flying down, driving, something. I can't hurt him. I hate being away from you." I too am independent, possess a life. . . .

Listening to my friend Harry talk as we drove up the coast I saw him more clearly than before. He had a trick of speech, knowing and cynical. He wished to be seen as richly unillusioned, an ironist. Facing up to the media, Harry said, how fine of you, God knows we've had enough naysaying.

It's not enough just accepting the modern world, it's a matter of total commitment by golly and if more people were total, Gordon, if more people followed your example—

The same tricks about California. Excitement was the name of the game, people talked this elitist rot, if there was only time enough to do justice to the place, really show it forth, the wonderful openness, flexibility, freshness, its rightness for people who wanted to live, the new active leisure. Harry's dinner-party-giving friend lived in the hills, and during the drive he ran on with ironic rhetoric and I felt removed from his knowingness, purified and simple. I looked out at the twilight and the white combers in the purple sea. Here and there we passed surfers standing by cars parked at the roadside. Boys and girls alike had yellow hair and orange skin, their wet waxed orange boards glistened in the washed air. A revolution in feeling, said Harry, staying with his self-protecting tone, a new way of addressing the world that actually is original. I felt a peculiar gentleness in my smiling silence. I thought: What a difference between talking about revolution—whether mocking it or otherwise—and feeling it! Mere knowingness—how empty it is! Unused to being at every moment aware I possessed a hidden life, a life like a tiny mad stolen masterpiece hung in a closet, a secret the thief hid almost from himself, I couldn't make a face that felt sincere. I felt oddly clubbable, equable, calm, as though I could be a priest to my friend and help him through his bitterness and negativism.

We turned off the highway into a pretty valley. Let's be fair, Harry explained. There was a California without tears

—at least some bits and pieces. Patches without sickly cheap popcorn and pizza and palm readers, bleeding eyes, hopheads, universal spiritual acne. . . . Let's Be Fair. The evening air was soft around us and there were small houses without boundaries or fences. Morgan horses roamed the open green fields, glowing mahogany lights. Some children were riding—they came close to the car, and Harry slowed down. They were bronze, barefoot, Indianlike on their mounts. They called out to each other and raced over a hillside out of sight and I heard their small quick cries coming from every direction as we drove on. A purple rained-on sunset light filled my eyes. I said it was beautiful. Harry's manner changed, eased. He explained that the people roundabout had opted out. Once they had been aircraft workers, some had small stakes of their own, they had bought the property and now they simply kept their land and horses, farmed a little, brought up their children to live outside and ride and enjoy the life, they worked irregularly and refused to play the game. As he spoke I thought I heard solid approval swell in his voice. Through my own mind a fantasy passed like a high shadow, a puff darkening some water. . . .

Maria, Harry's friend, lived atop a hill in a cinder-block house built by hand by a tormented script-writer in the thirties—the man's gesture of integrity. Great Danes huffed as the car came up the hill. A peacock strutted across the drive. In the garage an old Mercedes coupé sat next to a shiny scarlet sulky. Maria shouted at the dogs and took Harry into her arms. Inside, there were tapestries, velvet hangings, brass, Dutch chests, dim light, sideboards. A round bald clever-eyed man with deep-hued skin embraced Harry and led him away to talk before Maria introduced me. I talked to a movie director, a professor of French literature, a vintner. I felt remote and at peace with myself. Watching Harry with Maria and the others during dinner, I saw that Harry was treasured here. I realized—startled at my own generosity—that I was pleased for him. After the meal Maria came and talked to me. She had sculptured white hair, a smooth sun-darkened face. We like Harry, she said. But this terrible upside-down talk. Is he crazy? I said of course not, not even unhappy. The room grew quieter, and I listened to the voices, the fluencies, watched the night settling across the hills. My calm was spurious, I knew it to be, yet I was voluptuous in it. Where is she now? I thought. Has she eaten? *Rien du tout,* the round man said. My life is over, I don't ask questions. Why not? Harry said hotly. I felt the prickliness and impatience in his voice. The round man smiled apologetically as he talked. He wasn't wise-owling, he said. No arguing. No persuading. Accept, accept—the word had no meaning, of course. It wasn't even a joke. Activist, schmactivist, poison, pleasure—accept. It was the whole meaning of life and who could see it? Who would even want to see it?

"Serious stuff," Harry said, leaning out the car window to me. We were on the wrong side of the motel—I couldn't see Jean's lights. "I need you up on the bridge. Think about it. We can set it up tomorrow."

I realized I hadn't been listening on the long drive home. Harry had been talking about a job and I had simply shut off his voice.

"I'm serious," he said again. "Take it home and brood. I'll be in touch."

We shook hands and nodded strongly, man to man. Then he zoomed back to the Freeway and the (non?) revolution.

# 12

People began hurrying, worrying about the schedule. We had wasted time, we were behind, we were going to lose the truck and crew. The producer sat talking to himself at night about sticky zooms and wind noise, and gave jobs to Jean at midnight, insisted that she man the phone during breaks. . . . All at once time was becoming a problem for us. Yet I didn't think of the trip as coming to an end. I had stepped out of the project in my mind. The last day of shooting was marked in my book and return tickets were delivered but I was no longer thinking forward.

One morning during an editing break Jean and I were sitting beside the pool looking at the papers after breakfast. Jean left to dress. We were meeting each other downtown, she had shopping to do. A tape-truck man I didn't know who was sitting with us put down his paper and looked at me, grinning. He said how did I stand having two wives, wasn't it murder with one? "So don't tell me it's not my business. I didn't think they did this in Beantown, the Puritan stock." My face froze. I looked at the water. After a moment I stood up and dove into the pool and began doing laps. The sense of cowardice was still with me when I came out. The man was gone.

We met at a hotel. Cadillacs in jelly-bean shades lined the curb. I sat down to wait, and there was a frosting of thick yellow on my shoe tips—fuzz from the lobby carpet. Jean had been lucky. I saw her coming down a wide stairway and then toward me through a hallway and knew she was pleased with herself. Making appointments on the road was troubs, she had explained, but today she was lucky —somebody canceled. Her hairdo looked unnatural to my eyes, sweet disorder gone, no suggestive trace of dishevelment. I smiled as she came up, enjoying a vague condescension, something saddening and heavy and yet not unpleasant. We had drinks at the hotel, and riding back in the cab I noticed she was sitting apart, holding herself carefully, self-regardingly. It was odd to realize there was another way for her to look besides the ways I knew, and that it was this different way which she herself liked and valued. I felt relieved of a burden. I said that for the sake of her public relations it was time we ate supper with the others. She looked at me, then nodded. The producer and his wife and the others usually ate at the same place, and that night a dozen people were at the table. The producer's wife talked to me about her job. She had taken a job in the winter for a church organization that ran elegant boarding-houses for single girls, strangers to the city, and she spoke in a disdainful tone about rules and infractions that wound up on her desk. She told me she hadn't known whether "They" were serious when they invited her to play dean or housemother and punish people. I sensed her watching me, half-conscious slyness inside the disdain, but I listened and asked questions. Laughing with her, I took up hints she offered about the behavior of "her" girls. Now and then I looked across at Jean being amusing with Freddie and the others.

I lay beside her that night without touching her and talked in an even voice. Looking at the ceiling, I told her I worried about her. She hadn't eaten enough at dinner and she'd had a terrible lot to drink. Did this make sense? I went on quickly, not waiting for her to ask what I meant. I wanted her to listen to my voice and be reminded of facts without demanding explicitness. A tasteful reticence. I rose up on my elbows into the street light that came in the window. Minutes passed and Jean didn't speak. I began willing her to speak. I meant nothing, nothing, I told myself. I meant—

The phone rang. Jean took it in her living room. Her voice was effusive, embarrassed. She was laughing. Someone calling from abroad, Switzerland . . . but how'd you know where I was—but why, what time is it there? . . . How? Yes, of course. A week . . . New York, yes, well

maybe home . . . No she'd love to of course . . . of
course she wasn't mad . . . it's so nutty . . . you're an
idiot but of course not. I don't *mind,* don't be silly, very
flattering, yé-yé, blah-blah but this is costing mints, hang
*up,* idiot. . . . I was lying on the pillow when she came
back to the room. She lighted a cigarette and, with a small
sighing laugh, said oh what a lovely plant, how could it
have been better, and then explained that no it wasn't a
plant, no, believe it or not Rory was a boy who had been
proposing ever since she came out. He was abroad, a non-
profit economist for something, and he was coming home
and wanted to see her. He'd called her father in St. Louis,
didn't even think about the time, everybody loved him,
even her father, a tremendous athlete and not stupid really
. . . just sort of shockingly too kind.

There was a silence. I was looking at the ceiling, waiting
until I had the right control. I said: "You should take him."

My throat was dry. I wanted to laugh at myself but the
simple idea of so much feeling had caught me off balance.
Jean was in the doorway and then she was across the room
and on her knees beside me looking at me as though I was
hurt. She took my face in her hands, her fingers were like
petals and the sense of the harshness of my skin tortured
me. I did not look at her. I stood up and walked away from
her, burly, bearlike. I thought to myself: You are a grown
man. We held each other tenderly and lightly in the half-
darkness and whispered to each other instead of talking. In
time we began speaking aloud, yet in no normal tone,
gently, hesitantly, as though it were necessary to be tenta-

59

tive, as though we were convalescents nursing each other back toward the world. And as I drew her nearer and nearer to me, making her believe in my need, I felt a sapping process again inside me, energy-kill, powerlessness. I was a man ahead at a money game, cards or the wheel, yet certain to lose, a man alert to the coming downturn, yet waiting on helplessly, incapable of escape. But each time the chill of depression touched me, I moved my shoulders against it almost without thinking, for what could it possibly mean?

# 13

On the plane after the take-off we were like children. Jean had changed our flight and was girlishly self-congratulating about surprising me. We were leaving two whole hours ahead of the others, wowser, she explained. Double wowser, we were absolutely by ourselves. . . .

It was in fact hard to believe in this sudden gift of daylight freedom and privacy. Coming down the aisle I was restrained, wary—my eyes moved across faces ready to cut instantly free of Jean at a sign of recognition. We were in first class and the section was almost empty. We whispered together, our lips touching. Jean held my hand against her, and I felt the sweet full weight of her breathing. Despising my fear I turned zany. The stewardess smiled at us, and we ordered drinks without releasing each other, and when she left I slumped down, a comic, pretending to be slain by the stewardess's beauty. Jean bent over me and, our skin nerves rushing like beaten wind, we kissed in merriment beneath her sun-filled hair. We pretended to be sad for a moment, we told each other if we had had a weekend, if we had gone off just once . . . But then we caught each other up, realizing that this was not what we wanted. We did not want regrets, we did not want jokes. Yet jokes were what we had had and for a time we went through them again, laughing and yet feeling angry and frustrated at the laughter. We laughed at our staged exits and entrances from each other's apartments, at our staged happenings into each other. . . . We laughed at Red, the short-order cook who brought sandwiches to us by the pool and looked down at us like a priest with a blessing as we lay side by side in the sun. . . . We laughed about Kliegl's seal act in the pool, and I disproved that Kliegl was the hairiest man in the world. The thing is, it's not just an act, Jean said in her discreet-confidential-disclosure tone. Marty *is* a seal. We laughed at appetite, at our own appetites, at our own importunacy, resiliency. . . . Jean imitated my telling her I would be unable to perform and then rolled her eyes and spoke in her analyst-Viennese. . . . But then with no warning, her face softened, and I looked into her full eyes for a hundred miles without words. We drew apart from each other then, and Jean slept and I sat rigid, refusing every motion of my mind toward thought. The landing announcements came, and she lifted my hands and kissed them and pressed them against her and kissed them deeply again until she had no breath. But we sat apart still, no longer touching, looking away from each other into the whiteness coming down.

In a huge empty restaurant at O'Hare she slipped a folded piece of paper into my hand and then held my fingers tight. "I want to be a lady in a play," she began. "I want to be what you want." Then she stopped, she was squinting oddly. I reached out but she spoke quickly: "Don't make people look. I'm a lady in a play but I can't do it this minute. Wait just a minute." She sat for a second gathering herself as though she were catching her breath after running. She was frowning hard, her eyes shining. She spoke in a rush. "I wrote all the telephone numbers to everywhere but don't do it, please, it's only a week, we mustn't—" She looked past me, hesitating. "Oh sweetness—" she said suddenly and left me.

I had known we wouldn't go to her gate together. We had found a table with a view of the boarding area so that both of us would know where to look when her plane was leaving. Jean had decided not to go back to her apartment during the break. She was visiting her parents in St. Louis. She had been talking inconsequentially about her father. He had had a heart attack, it enraged him not to be able to play a full round of golf. I listened, feigning concern. I wanted to stop her from talking and explain precisely who and what I was, how I could not *be* this, how— It was then that she gave me the piece of paper. Another minute and she was gone.

There were three planes in the boarding area, placed so that I couldn't be certain which was hers. The plane nearest me blocked the view of people boarding, and it was the last to leave. Only when all three were up and I had followed them intently until nothing winked in the sky did I return to myself. I thought of my eyes and my face as they would be seen and cleared them of intensity and fear. Gazing out the wide window, Muzak in my ears as the waiter came toward me to take away Jean's glass and the cigarette rubble, I felt a quiver of defiance. I frowned at the window and called out loud for the check. I remembered afterward, a thousand miles nearer my place, how small my voice sounded in that room, thin, unconfident, ill-at-ease. A matter of acoustics only, heavy carpets, curtains, padded white linen simply blotting the sound of me up.

# 14

"She's a bitch," my wife said that night at supper. "He's so used to it he didn't say a word. Why would anybody want to *be* that mean?

"She knew exactly what day it was," my wife said. "They had to bring presents for the wishing well, she remembered about that. It's true, she's a bitch. She expects boys to act like darling little girls."

I nodded understandingly. I felt relaxed and easy. From the first minute, my first gazing down, first touching, false gladness in my eyes, I saw there was no way for truth to be read in me. There was no lie in me as I appeared to others. I could relax, I was utterly safe. At once I wished I did not know this, and I listened more intensely to put the knowledge out of my mind. My wife was bringing me up to date. Putting me in the picture. She spoke as though I had never been gone. I watched her at a distance, curiously. She was angry at a teacher—the younger boy's teacher. The teacher had kept him after school and it was Fair Day, rides and booths on the Common, Ferris wheel, the Whip, children looked forward for weeks, mean to keep anybody in, how could she do it! Feelings stirred lazily inside me, leaves in a mild breeze. Pity, forgiveness . . . I didn't allow myself to move back into memory but I sat heavily, luxuriantly, weighted with an untouched but touchable secret fortune.

"—he didn't want to bring it in," said the voice in the room, "that's how upset he was. I found it in his saddlebag. He wasn't going to say a word. 'I wish you wouldn't be so careless,' " my wife imitated the singsong of the teacher too broadly. I was embarrassed, I felt myself assessing the matter as though no child of mine were involved. " 'I told you not to be so careless about your writing and spelling and punctuation, it's all mistakes and I'm giving you S minus.' There couldn't *be* anything better in her class and there she was—"

I felt my wife's anger and realized I wasn't responding in my usual way. I had failed to make a speech on the difficulties that parental anger could create. My gospel of moderation and control—I saw it now as a lying ploy. All I cared about—it was true, was it not?—all I cared about was preventing confrontations. Embarrassments. My advocacy of control, my representations of "the other point of view"—they were meaching. I hadn't the courage of my feelings.

My wife had this courage. If she felt like defending her sons, she defended them, regardless of the enemy. I sat listening in patronizing admiration. I knew this view of my wife's directness only meant I had stepped farther away from her. But didn't she grasp that herself? How could she be oblivious?

"I'll go see the lady," I said firmly, cheerfully. "We'll set her straight." From the pantry, pouring a second brandy, I called out to her to tell me some more.

Midnight, church bells. The face opposite me glanced down, consulted a watch, looked up, looked past me. I read the expression cruelly. Familiar, expectant, persuadable, game. Warmth on my face, satanic innerness. As steps went up the stairs another church bell, farther off . . . I shut the cat in the cellar and put away bottles and closed the phonograph in my study. I turned the lights out in the kitchen—then turned them back on abruptly. A Koda-chrome postcard was pinned to the bulletin board, swimming pool, palm trees—

> The X is my room. I take a swim every morn-
> ing before breakfast. Never a rainy day. Pres-
> ents coming in mail. Remember what I said.
> Record players down, etc. Home soon, love—
>
> Dad

My temples beat hard as I stood with the thing in my hand. My face was hot. I shook my head at myself in a rush of self-scorn. I saw myself climbing the carpeted staircase like an actor in a set—a cutaway stage, a missing wall that let others look at the actor as he looked in on his children in their sleep, let people watch him "loving them all the more," caring far more than "before." Pathos, falsity . . . Without thinking I put the tack into the board and slipped the card into my pocket. Changing my face once more I looked around me again inspectingly, hesitating in order to break into the tide of self-disgust in my thoughts. Then I turned off the light and went up to our room.

# 15

In the morning after breakfast the boys and I worked outside. The yard was coming apart. Flagstones grassed over, spikes of grass in the brick walks, elm trees up through the cellar window grates, clipping undone, bittersweet tangled under the porch roof, a storm had knocked down the wisteria wires . . . I worked without thinking, enjoying the heat, stopping now and then to empty the lawn sweeper or to throw a stick for the dog. Waiting for him to fetch I felt my palms gritty inside my cloth gloves and the slick dampness on my skin. I thought of the movement of muscle in my arms, I thought of my "condition." After a bout with the clippers I sat back on the porch roof grinning down at my staff. Father of two sons. Provisioner. Coper. I was no other man but this—wet, gritty, workaday, fatherly, amused. The older lad looked up at me from the mower and waved over the noise of the machine. They hate jobs, I thought, liking the moment, but at that they know that not having jobs is worse. . . . Down from the roof, I rolled Robespierre over and spent a quarter of an hour hunting and cracking fleas.

Toward noon we went off with lunch to a meadow pond back from the highway on a cart road that goes into the hills. We had the place to ourselves. Springy and deep, pure for the pure. The sun was high, the grass smelled of it. The boys poled up the shallows on a raft with their mother. I lay in the sun and savored the idyl. Part of my life is this. It is real. This is real water. The voices down the water are real voices, the shadows that move are the shadows of their bodies. . . . In a while I was burning. I threw myself in and let the black freezing water close over me. I came up splashing the boys as they swung out on the jungle rope from a tree, measuring their own crashing dives. Birds scuttered in the shadows as I dried myself. I closed my eyes and fell asleep.

We stopped for corn at the farm on the way home and afterward I sat in my study alone for a time. I sat over a passbook and a broker's statement, adding and subtracting. . . . A part of me knew what I was doing but I avoided thinking of my purpose. Before I left my desk I tore up my calculations carefully into small pieces and put them into the wastebasket, at the bottom.

The boys were eating supper by themselves when I came

out. My wife was nowhere. A sudden clamor of fear inside me—I stood staring, wordless, at them. The boys laughed. Had I forgotten something? They reminded me about a party, we were going out—a neighborhood party. When they finished clearing I took the younger boy outside and warmed him up slowly and easily in the smooth evening air. . . . The evening was warm. My wife came to the door once calling out for the cat. Her voice was fluty and sweet. Children's sounds echoed over the lawns, dogs barking, the slack and smack of the ball and glove. The boy was faster, I realized, his pitches were heavier in the mitt. When he was warm, I brought him inside and sat on the bed while he explained team problems from the tub. His hair was wet and cool, he stood naked holding my shoulders as I clipped his toenails. When he was in his pajamas, cool fresh thin transparent cloth, I kept him in front of the mirror, meaning to show him something about his motion. He had grown bigger, I realized in surprise, visibly taller and broader—he had physically grown in the time I had been away. I read a story and put him in, ruffling his hair with my hand, telling him to keep the ball low in the game. Let them hit.

I made myself a dressing drink and then as I came back upstairs music started in the living room—the older boy and his Group. I paused on the landing. The heavy stroke of the bass guitar shook the air. It excited me. I smiled, remembering Jean telling me why she wanted to go home, not straight to New York. I heard her voice saying, "I'll just go sit and think and think and never stop thinking.

They're so nice. They go out and they ask me and I can just say Oh I'm tired, I think I'll sit and think. They're awfully nice. I have the whole house, lots of peace. 'Great.' " The musicians stopped. I heard them talking. I could see in my imagination my younger son trying to catch the words, up on his elbows from his pillow straining to listen. I felt again a faint pity for Jean alone in an empty house. My son called out from his room. "He's all hot," the boy said as I opened the door. The poodle was sitting on the boy's stomach. "He stinks." I laughed and the dog barked. My wife called out to me. The dog was licking my hand and the boy was halfway down the stairs as the music began again.

# 16

In New York the weekend before the second series script talks my wife shopped and I went with her or spent time walking in and out of galleries. When I wasn't with her, when I was looking at pictures or whatever I did, I saw her goodness in my thoughts. The separateness of this seeing— who will believe the pain it brought? Cold loneliness . . . Sitting beside her when she was shopping for herself, waiting for dresses or coats to be brought out. No visible nervousness at first. I would feel at most—concentration. Inarticulateness. Preoccupation around the eyes. She was being condescended to for plainness from some sleazy shoplady stupidity, and she didn't notice, that was the point. I sat watching her considering "wrong things" without being dismissive of them. Because to be dismissive meant saying that choosing an article of clothing was significant and that she was like everyone else, like millions who became somebody by wearing this or buying that. Because this was the price she believed (unconsciously, but that didn't matter) must be paid to avoid humiliating herself or someone else. I never helped her, I only listened and watched. What could I have done? She was happy buying soldiers or pajamas for the boys, she enjoyed herself at counters where there was no contest, where she could speak and look unself-consciously and make her mind up at ease. Her character was rooted in a knowledge of true values. She cared for the genuine. She was beyond vanity. It was actually a trouble for her to think of herself.

We were nearly the last people to sit for lunch in our restaurant but no one was impatient. My wife was abstracted at first, looking around the room, fussing about eating something "fancy" or exotic. For a minute or two there were the hints of a "proper" posture, an appropriate elegance. Standing off from it, seeing it plainly, I felt shame. Cheerfulness and then the raffishness born in midafternoon wine spoke in her soon and she found her confident laughing voice and talked to busboy and waiter as though they weren't strangers but Conroy the postman. She abused the ridiculous snobs found in every corner of the city. I smiled approvingly from my distance, judgmental, sober. Candor, generosity, givingness . . . Later in a china store I stood and listened while she and a salesman labored the truth that nowhere in New York could you confidently and reasonably get table knives repaired that had been ruined in the dishwasher. We Boston people were fortunate to have somebody still doing things as a matter of course. . . . In the early evening, looking at the TV while she enjoyed her "favorite luxury," a hot uninterrupted bath, I thought: She is a mother. Her life is my children. She will give everything. She will press herself to the last hurt, laughing at her own willingness and yet without hesitation—

In a movie we saw that weekend an Englishman of fifty becomes infatuated with an eighteen-year-old Irish girl. The scenes in which the two made love gripped me in the chair. I wanted to cry out sharing their joy. I was aware of my face smiling up at the screen, almost speaking with it. By the column of light I turned to look at my wife. Her eyes were bright, gleaming. She was entranced. I dropped my glance, cut the cord of involvement, detached myself from the figures on the screen. On the street afterward I felt old. I held my wife's arm as we walked. Yes, I said. I did enjoy it. Yes I loved the girl. I said then the words that poisoned my sense of myself for an hour. I said, But what was it, really, nothing but the usual quick little sex fantasy. My wife looked rueful but quite agreed.

# 17

"It won't play," Norton Ginsbury the writer said, fitting a filter cigarette into his Sano holder. "Fuck it. It won't play because it won't play."

"Check," said Kliegl. "By the way—"

I said for the third time we weren't thinking pictures yet, and Freddie nodded mildly. The river in the window did not move. There was nothing in my mind except Jean. Anybody seen Jean? My inner ear tested the words. Could I say this lightly? Heavily, mockingly, any tone, whatever you want . . . Where's Jean anyway? The week's over, why isn't she here? Punishing somebody? Forget it, forget it . . . The river was deep blue in the morning light. I walked piers on Saturday when I was in college, riding the trolley and walking on a Saturday morning past dock sheds where the air was spongy with fruit and oil smell and the ships' fat leaded smokestacks lay in so close they seemed to rub the roofs. A liner was coming in, blinding white, black barges creeping, a freighter dragging deep in the current, a strip of cream at the bridge. . . . Kliegl was still talking. The first trip I made to New York was a bus ride. Yes, Mother, I'm coming back, yes it's safe, yes I've got money, yes I'm missing school, no I'm not missing a thing. . . . At noonday I sat and watched the soot swarming in the new light. Girls came out from John Street and William Street down Broadway and I was sitting at the Battery watching the ferries brushing little silent waves like white blossoms ahead of them, gulls clacking. . . .

"Shit," the writer said. "I'm just winging it, wait'll I finish."

"Who wants corn beef?"

"—'but I had formerly been a great lover of fish,' " Freddie read aloud, trying something I'd passed him, " 'and when this came hot out of the frying pan it smelled admirably well. I balanced some time between principle and inclination till I recollected that when the fish were opened I saw smaller fish taken out of their stomachs. Then thought I: if you eat one another, I don't see why we mayn't eat you. So I dined upon cod very heartily. . . . So convenient a thing it is to be a reasonable creature, since it enables one to find or make a reason for everything one has a mind to do.' "

Freddie flicked his stop watch and looked at it.

"Twenty-three seconds," he said. "Frankly I think it's kind of cute."

"I like a concept," the writer said. "I can't write with a lot of fucking ideas in my head though."

People murmured. Somebody opened a folder and began passing envelopes around the table. Schedules, tickets. There was a sandwich in front of me and I bit into it angrily. I got up, waving at them thickly, excusing myself. . . .

"Doctor F.?" She was standing in the production-room doorway. The breath rushed into my lungs. Her face was pale. She was tired. She was very tall. She was taller than my memory knew. Her figure was completely unemphasized. She wore a green dress with a light-green border from neck to hem and a small bow at the waist. I had not seen it before. She leaned against the doorway, her feet crossed in her way. There were papers in her hand.

"It's looking very well. They had me in the library all day."

I had no words.

"Come to my house for a drink. I'll introduce you to yummy Donna. Yummy Donna and Teddie. It'll be Swell."

I looked at her.

"The other side of the museum, ten minutes. Darling, run, won't you? Can't you run?"

She was gone. I felt the words I called out ending somewhere away from me up the hall.

"Throw flowers." The black girl at the switchboard

grinned up at me through the glass. She nodded at Jean's doorway. "She even lends money."

I smiled. Music sounded. The girl called out laughingly, pointing behind me. At the end of the row the Muzak elevator was waiting. I turned and ran.

# 18

We placed ourselves like strangers in the cab. I didn't touch her, barely looked at her. We were locked into public feelings—self-consciousness, pretended formal amusement. When I saw Jean in the doorway the one impulse in me was—to shake her hand! I wanted to disavow our bodies, clear myself of lust? Jean began talking in the cab at a pitch that was wrong. She talked about her roommate. Donna had finally gotten engaged and the boy was a perfectly nice boy and it would be lovely having Donna out of the house at last and, marvy, they weren't going to wait forever, because Teddie had a foreign job or something, but the thing was they would be there, inevitably they would be there and-and-and it was a question how quickly they could be gotten away from there and where was I staying and could we possibly eat, she wasn't asking anybody to be stupid but there was a small place two blocks up Second, quite off the track in a way. . . .

Her house was on 76th Street. The doorman greeted her in effusions. He didn't look at me. A small bristly gritty man in a stained brown brass-buttoned jacket. Jean called him Timmy and was controlled and maternal with him, talking about weather. I smiled without meeting the man's eye. The ring boxes in the vestibule were rusted and the lobby was small and dark. She pressed her own buzzer and led me down a corridor past dark Spanish wood chairs, high-backed, up a few stairs to her mailbox, up another flight to her floor. To my eyes the place was dark, dirty, airless. I looked back upon myself entering, looked back at the chairs, the stucco walls, looked back upon that as though I were passing through a mythic place—house of Single Girl, hostess of Older Man. At the doorway before she put the key in the lock she looked at me and smiled and said soundlessly with her lips: Be Nice.

Roommate and fiancé were opening packages in the hallway. As I was introduced I felt the young man drop down behind his eyes. The sight was not relaxing. The couple went on opening letters, packages—the girl read a sentence aloud here and there, congratulatory words. Jean showed me the liquor closet and I followed her into the kitchen. Our voices could not be heard here but we spoke as though standing before thousands. I was filled with a sense of absurdity as I moved about the kitchen, and again as I sat with Jean in her living room. A grown man among children. The place punished me. There in the hallway sat a couple, strangers to me. The couple sat and discussed, in affectedly casual, condescending tones, gifts from their elders—aunts, well-wishers. I was punished. My temples ticked as we tried to speak. I was punished, forced to speak as though overheard by others, though I knew the others were rigorously not listening. I could not look at Jean, I could not sit back. It was a return to adolescent dependency. I could not touch her until they were gone, therefore touching, kissing, grasping, copulating were emptied of freedom and meaning, they were rituals, forbiddennesses. Humiliating to turn backward in time and pretend to an ease one did not possess. Ridiculous to let it go on forever.

Nothing changed when they left. Nothing changed as we walked together, as I took her arm. The humiliation of furtiveness, then of a pretended recklessness that came down to nothing more than a refusal to look about me as I walked, a refusal to heed faces we passed. I was with Jean and not with her, I was not thinking of her, I was thinking of being watched, being seen. In the restaurant, after a half hour, I let my eyes go round the room, confronting faces that ignored me. I meant not to let Jean see me do this. A cold ingenuity allowed me to look toward her, to look into her and seem to have no other possible object within my vision. Yet I was taking in tables adjacent, movements in the room, figures entering. I lied to her with my eyes, with my face that expressed joy in my nearness to her, exhilaration, naturalness, ease.

In the hotel elevator a calm settled over us, we spoke quietly, we spoke without turning to each other, I felt us turning iron, distant. Behind the door, I crushed her to me, crying aloud. On the bed when I touched her silken crotch she was instantly wet and we tore at each other wildly, clothes strewn round us and were clumsy, grappling mouth on mouth, collapsing, whispering hotly in her ear oh come be fucked, Jeanie sweet, fuck me, and collapsing we threw ourselves back powerless and empty on the bedclothes, too dizzied, breathless, exhausted, too shocked at ourselves to touch.

# 19

I woke that night into blackness. I lay quiet for a time, breathing softly and not stirring, hearing the faint voices of traffic in the street far below. A taxi horn darted an arrow into the dark air. I felt troubled, in doubt. . . . Lifting my arm—reaching out for her. Nothing. I jerked myself upright in the darkness and touched my hands down wildly over the bed. The moonlight showed me nothing. I shouted. It was like a cry in a horror movie, long and shrill and I made it longer. I stood up breathing wildly in the darkness. Weird thoughts struck at me. I had killed her? Was I a murderer? A madman? I'd simply had a dream, everything. . . . I ran to the door whimpering and turned on the overhead light.

Her note was on the night table.

*Darling, you're sleeping so beautifully and I have to go now and I don't want to wake you. Call me in the morning the minute you can, the minute you wake. Dearest, dearest, sweet dreams—*

I sank onto the bed, feeling lifeless and yet aware of myself, aware of something in my mind seizing on the note, making it yield a meaning. . . . I held it flat on my knee, studied it, peering through my blindness, remembering myself shrieking in terror— It had been a shriek, nothing less— It was unfeigned terror, was it not? Why had it taken me so, overmastered me? What did it mean? I realized I was still quite literally breathless.

I sat shaking my head, conscious of the melodramatics of shaking my head. Of course, of course. She had to think of Donna. Donna would wonder if she was very late, wonder and worry and draw fresh conclusions and possibly gossip to Teddie? Not to friends, but to Teddie? It was clear to me, but even as I sat on the edge of the bed aware of my extravagance, I could not stop thinking I had touched my depth. A force had shot through me, torn me out of myself, made me shout and whimper in terror for her, fear she was gone. There was a depth in me, an intensity beyond anything I could believe or predict. It asserted itself on its own, no prompting, no false stimulation. It wasn't a thought, not an acted thought, nothing that had to do with showing forth, or with making or leaving impressions. . . . Before I knew what actually happened, before I knew she was gone, that she left only a note, that I hadn't been dreaming, I had nevertheless known everything in my feelings. The idea that there was so much truth in me, a depth that ripped a cry of fear from me involuntarily, the idea I had become, even for an instant, a man of premonitions, turned me grave, made my hands heavy. It was like a birth. . . .

I gave her number in a deliberate voice to the night operator, glancing at my watch with a recording impassive interest. It was 2:00 A.M. There were voices at the other end when the receiver was picked up—girls' voices. Children. Jean spoke. I talked to her slowly, heavily, in a humorless, unimagining, unwitty voice, pressing my words down as though they were forms laid on wax. I told her I had not known where she was. I told her that waking up in the empty room—it had shown me something. It told me the state of my feelings. I had been that terrified only once before. Had she known I would have felt this way, even for a moment, no matter how trivial in essence she thought the "thing" as she called it between us to be, she would not have wanted it. The flip words, sweet dreams, they were like slugs, they had no substance, she would be ashamed even if she meant to tell me something, she would be ashamed of having written them—she would be ashamed, that is, if she knew how wide the gap was between her tone and the feelings within me when I woke up. Yes oh yes, it was panic, yes ridiculous— Yes it was crazy, absolutely, and of course I heard the smiling voices in the background, a mockery of the voice she heard in her ear. Yes it was a shower for Donna, midnight entertainment, an obligation —I wouldn't ask, didn't want to know, of course I was ridiculous. I didn't care or mind, this was what I was calling her to say, I didn't care. All that mattered was that she had acted as though she had a life of her own separate from mine, and that cry that seized me, that in fact wakened me, told me she didn't have this right. It had all turned. I didn't any longer know what I wanted to say to her, but she did not have this life she thought she had, her life was mine and if she couldn't bear it, couldn't stand knowing it, then . . .

It was still black night when she knocked. I opened the door and she looked at me, her eyes were humorous, sheepish, full. I thought of speaking, telling her I knew the humiliations, had imagined even the lubricious eyes turned on her, cabdriver, elevator man. . . . I hadn't wanted this, hadn't asked her to come back, didn't expect . . . I said nothing. We kissed, not touching with our hands. We made love in a strange dutiful weary wordless touching way and dressed and in the black dawn walked thirty blocks toward her street. Now and then I repeated, as though talking to myself, Something's changed, something's happened. I had felt something change inside myself. She looked away. Our hands did not touch. We agreed that while there was sadness at the surface now, there was another kind of feeling below. It had no name. It was simply—strong. Now and then we turned to each other, not to kiss but to study each other detachedly as we walked. We stopped once suddenly and clasped each other tight in the entrance to a store, not speaking, caught in a puzzle of feeling. I felt that someone looking on at us would be certain to see this as momentous, fearful. We drank coffee, sitting on counter stools in a First Avenue sandwich shop, and picked up the *Times,* and looked at it desultorily, scornfully. People were coming out of her apartment house when we came near there, men with traveling days ahead. My eyes were drawn and tight and I felt the bristling on my cheeks and the squalor of my shirt—I felt them as proofs, testimony of the strength of that cry that shouted through me in the blackness. I waited while she left a note for Donna to call them at work, and then she came back with me in a cab to the hotel and we lay together for hours with the blinds drawn discovering each other freshly, holding each other, touching everywhere with our fingers, mouths, making a love that had no accents, no beginning, no crises, no endings. . . .

I went back by train for the slowness. In the station we walked together halfway up the platform and now I truly was heedless of others. I said that because I had no sleep I couldn't control myself, she would have to leave me here or I couldn't go on without— She put my hand to her lips and left me. I watched from the door of the car, she turned once with her hand upraised as though to wave but her hand only moved in the air, a candle guttering. She went on slowly. Inside the car I sat for a time with my eyes tightly closed. When I could safely open them I leaned my head back into the filth of the chair and fell into a deep undreaming sleep, and when the conductor woke me I rose up with the full memory of terror, an aloneness, at my throat. The man stepped back from me and said, Hold on, recovering, smiling. Hold on. It's all right, friend, it's all right. Relax.

# 20

"Who is she?" my wife said again. "Was she in California? I'm sorry. I'll stop."

We were both lying on our backs. There was a full moon in the window. I hadn't said a word, had "admitted" nothing. I felt her breathing beside me. Her voice came into the silence slowly, gropingly, a voice in a dream.

"The problem is taking it in. It's too hard. I don't understand, I honestly don't. People have something that's perfect, unique— They have happiness and hope— I'm not just being stupid and wifely. Why does it happen? Does anybody know why it happens?"

I said that nothing was happening. I said it was getting late.

"We never did this before either, did we. Drawing back like this. I was never closed out. I've been closed out."

She sat up and looked at the moon in the window. She was frowning.

"It's not insulting," she said. Her voice was very intent on its reasoning. "I never would have guessed. I couldn't have thought—that's the point of course. You can't predict what you'll feel. It's not the humiliation, I'm positive of that. Blame the Puritans. It's the waste I think about. It's unbelievable people can waste so much . . ."

"—the boys were just coming back from tennis," my wife said. The moon was gone. "I was in the garden weeding. I heard them put their bikes down and I was just about to call out and then all of a sudden it happened. I couldn't speak. All of a sudden I was sitting on my bottom in the sunshine crying. They came looking for me and stood there staring. I must have looked crazy— I caught myself, I didn't say anything. I said, no, I was temporarily feeling sad about nothing and go get the clippers, wouldn't they. But it was amazing. I'd known everything for weeks—you were gone, I was losing you. . . . It never happened inside me though—that was it. Then wham. I just felt made of water. Chrissie was holding onto my shoulder and Jere said, Come on come on come on. They were so embarrassed for me—" She waited a moment. In the darkness I imagined her eyes remembering. "I was sitting there getting myself organized, teary and a mess. It was unreal. I stopped thinking about us. I was thinking about them. Jere's such a sweet kind little boy, his sweet little face— It's true, I've always said that about them both. They're both kind and good. . . ."

"I'm scared in so many ways it's like hysteria," my wife said. The sky had lightened out the window. "Which way do I run? I'm scared I'm a coward, scared I won't have any courage, scared of waiting for you to tell me, scared for somebody else to tell me. 'Oh I'm so sorry, Mattie, I thought you knew about her, Gordon's woman—' It's the idea of waiting and waiting and then at last it's out and you have to talk. You're going to have to talk, don't you see? You can't just not speak and lie there awake. I'm not being bitchy. I'm being truthful. Sooner or later we're going to have to talk. You're going to have to say something. Don't you see there isn't any other way?"

# 21

Plans month came—it is a hectic time in my office because of the government, and there was less for me in New York. I didn't nag myself. Talking with accountants and section heads I felt efficient, crisp of mind. In the morning mirror, lathering my face, I saw health and freshness and physical force. I swung my arms as I walked, called out teasing greetings on the way to my cubicle. The people around me, partners, staff—I felt warm toward them. They deserved pity and kindness. When they acted as though unaware that this alone was their due, only then could I be impolite. Often in meetings I rose in impatience, walked around the table. I'd notice the shape of my partners' heads, the dryness of the skin on their necks. . . . Were they truly content to be here? They asked nothing of life? They believed they were living their lives? I was exhilarated by sudden darting clarities of vision—this man's self-regard and self-flattery, that man's emptiness, sad insignificance. . . . Here were my co-workers, proud of their inventiveness, delighting in their power to separate mickey mouse from wit, sure of their ability to judge, distinguish. . . . They were proud to be what they were. . . . Why? How could they care about the work? Over and over the same feelings, the same questions . . . Someone returned from vacation—tanned face, glowing, pleased, sense of specialness in the eyes. I thought: what you've done is pointless. I knew it was too easy—this diminishing of others, this "understanding" that time spent by others was unreal, delusive. But there was no meanness or preening in it. I perceived the emptiness of other lives neutrally, coolly. . . . A predictable compound.

Always there was her voice. We talked on the telephone. In the morning Jean called from her office and spoke briefly and tersely, as though reporting. "Good morning, Doctor." "Good morning, Miss. Miss Hollis, isn't it?" "That is correct, Doctor." "Did Miss Hollis sleep well?" "Doctor, this is a business call, this call is monitored." "Sorry." "I was once in love but I've forgotten the man's name." "Miss Hollis, please—" "A large v. grainy man. Doctor, could I be losing my mind?" "The thought comes, Miss Hollis." I called from pay telephones, and my pockets were heavy with telephone change. I called from the pay phone in the cellarway of my building, hearing my voice echo up the stairwell, a janitor talking outside, and nevertheless I talked on and on and hung up and waited in the booth and paid the extra minutes and waited again for her to call back. She would not let me say good-bye. I'm so cheap, I pursue you. Shameless, she said. I won't let you say it. Let me say it, no, don't go. Hang up and I'll call back. Oh of course I'll eat, I promise, but darling, don't go, don't go. She called me in the cellarway. Call me back in the telephone near the men's room, the cocktail lounge of the motel, no I can't describe it, don't be crazy. All right, it has blowers that blow your hands dry. Call me back at a cemetery monument lot, per-petual care . . . There were frequent small surprises, calls late at night, sudden chances. . . . I would stand in the lighted booth, my back to the roaring road, waiting for her midnight voice to come across the darkness to me, sleepy, questioning, rich in certainty that I alone would speak. When I left the booth, turned away, my shoulders were all command and resigned force.

And then lying beside her, lying in Jean's bed in Jean's white bedroom, her coolness along my legs, hearing her talk of Donna's pending departure and her uncertainty about having the place to herself in the future, hearing still in my ears the extraordinary piercing music of her cry of love one moment before, oh my God, my darling, how you— Oh my *dar*ling— Hearing all this, holding her in my arms, rich beyond imagining, no equaling my fortune, I believed there could not be a time for any talk but this, everything must wait, I will plan, think, arrange, work out, I thought, clenching my mind, gritting it, but not now not now not now.

# 22

A moment: I arrive early and unannounced at Jean's house. It is Sunday. We are to meet at Kennedy and fly out from there, but I come in early and take a cab to the city, stopping a block from her house. The cab moves away and I am alone on the walk. I see myself as an agent scouring a life, prowling "byways." The neighborhood will "tell me something."

It's midmorning and already fiercely hot. Someone is coming toward me—a man with a dog. I stand at the curb watching abstractedly. I may or may not be waiting for just this man. He has a goatee, he wears an open-necked shirt and Alpine shorts. The dog is a borzoi. The man meets my eye, and the irritableness of the glance tells me I've been staring. I drop my glance, cough to hide my embarrassment. I face away from Jean's house, walking slowly. The fancy grocery, the liquor store—I remember Jean cashed a check for me here. It occurs to me—I could bring flowers. I look about for a florist. There are several on the street, all closed. I'm perspiring, I feel aimless. What am I doing? A grown man, father of sons . . . My wife sits drinking Sunday-morning coffee in our garden, knowing— But it's only superstition. She knows nothing. She can't see me standing here, looking at nothing, looking into a dress-shop window, looking away from glances when none is directed at me. Eleven-thirty A.M. Sunday. Lunacy . . . But suppose it's a matter of my being the kind of man who has more feeling, more desire, more need to live? Is this idea arrogance? Fantasy?

Abruptly I turn about, going now in the direction of Jean's house. Again I stop. I check myself. Best to call, of course. Give some warning. Donna will be there. Timmy the doorman. The man with the brass buttons that turned green. Timmy approved of me. Timmy hadn't ever liked Rory, for instance, but Dr. Flint—imprimatur. In my memory I hear Jean telling me this, saying that Timmy always has opinions about her escorts, people who come by. I think now: She was telling me she had a life before me. I think: Is it innocence that makes her believe in the caring protective doorman? Is it fear? I feel a rush of anger at whatever frightens her. But at once in my imagination I'm back in the lobby, standing at the buzzer, waiting for her to ring back, whereupon Timmy appears. What do I say? Morning, lovely day, hot, hot . . .

The heat shatters windows around me, blazing and booming. I'm dizzy in the phone booth, listening to the ringing. But those who can't see themselves in my place—they're less than I, aren't they? They don't weigh as much?

And what softness and kindness, what curling yielding kindness, in Jean's voice! How my heart soars, how swiftly all doubt's gone. Donna's away! Jean cries. I hear her delight. She's away on a weekend, forget the flowers, just come, I'm packing, I'm out of my head, dearest dearest dearest, we'll ride out, aren't you beautiful . . . I walk briskly through the terrible heat and ring her buzzer and go through the door conscious of no darkness or drabness. There's no doorman on. Jean teases me at the door, eying me through the round glass. Sorry, no peops, just chix . . . And she's in my arms.

But in an instant everything's difficult again. Strained, uneasy. We're not going to make love.

We aren't going to make love, therefore we are neither before nor after making love. We're simply before—a trip. Before finishing packing. Her apartment swelters. The air conditioner has collapsed, she and Donna use an exhaust fan in the kitchen when this happens. In theory it pulls used air out and allows fresh air to come in the living-room windows. Science. Jean is packing. I feel myself intruding into domesticity and routine. Her place isn't charming seen this way. Her pictures aren't as striking as at night. Timid colors . . .

Why should it matter whether anything's good or bad?

Yet there's still truculence in the air. . . . Something—

When there is no love, no passion, no thought of touching, too hot, too little time before the plane . . . What then are we? I sit with the thin summer *Times* in my hand asking myself, What are we? Nothing substantial, is that right? Empty? I sit on the couch with the paper on my knees and time stretches longer and longer without words. Jean is in the bedroom. I begin calling out to her in my mind, my forehead dripping, my hands sweating and grimy. I call out to her in my mind to say something. Say something, please Jean. Speak. I stand up quickly, dumping the paper on the floor—I'm near despair—and go into her room. She looks up from the suitcase—but I'm staring at myself. Somewhere she's found a picture of me! She picks it up from the night table and looks at it consideringly. "Freddie helped me, he thought it was for a joke." Her eyes are witty, brimming. I am *moved*—strongly, suddenly moved. I lift her in my arms, I lift her and place her on the bed, stand above her looking down, wordless.

"Guess what, ducks," she says laughing, bringing me down to her, "we're going to miss the plane," and I do not speak. I only look into her, very close to her, staring, and *I cared too much and I was a fool,* my wife's voice wakes in my brain, *It's my fault and I'm a fool.*

A moment: Jean's sister's house outside Baltimore. White brick, black shutters, boxwood, white wrought iron, a greenhouse, a court, a pool . . . Behind the hedge a cutting garden, a vegetable garden, a guest cottage, an unobstructed view to the south. Pausing at a gate Jean says she loves the house, it is her favorite house in the world. I understand I am to see the fondness of her elder sister and well-off brother-in-law as competing with mine, she wishes to seem more valuable in my eyes, someone thought of, cosseted, never alone. . . . My cynicism and its clarities again sadden me and I turn distant. By careful purpose I miss out family nicknames, am cool to Jean's sister through my politeness. I float on a mattress, taking the sun in front of the pink-shuttered pool house while Jean and her sister talk, and try to force darkness away, but over and over— Wrong things occur in series. Yes, I call out, answering their question, yes I'd like a drink and will make it myself. Heeding her sister's commands about cabinets and ice in the pool-house kitchen, hearing the commonplace voice saying the Bloody Mary in the jug is famous in these parts, I feel unamusedly aware of the gap between this sense of me, this apparent understanding of my nature, my occupation, my standing in my own eyes—a male free of a weekday, pouring iced vodka dripping in the sun—and the facts.

And worse when Jean's brother-in-law drives up with the children, blond sons, fresh-skinned, tanned. The brother-in-law's affable, easy, talks about drinks and golf as though I were there daily, will be there tomorrow. The children aren't shy but I can't look at them. This is Dr. Flint, Jean says, and he'll cut you dead if you don't say Gordon. I look past their ears. I feel myself nodding, the silence won't end inside me. I hear birdsong in the stillness, feel the yardman in the garden on the other side of the hedge. I do not even smile.

After the parting we drive a full half hour on the highway before either of us speaks.

Jean says: "Why did I do that? Really. Why did I want to do that?"

*Do you remember the mice in the wastebasket in the monastery? You wouldn't get out of bed.*

I feel her not looking at me because she is nearly frightened to do so and I flail at myself for my distance, my coldness. I feel her aware of my not lifting my shoulders, not helping her, not letting my eyes leave the road.

She puts her head back, closes her eyes. When we are in mid-city, she speaks again. "They thought they knew. They think they know all about it and they haven't got the right to think. They haven't got the right to sit and talk about us. What do they know?"

*I remember every room in every house we ever had.*

I let the silence stretch between us because I am thinking as I listen. Everyone is speaking at once. Yes, I say, they *are* talking about us and I can hear exactly what they say.

Again: we're in a restaurant in a river town in Missouri, asbestos shingles outside, bar, knotty pine, candlelight, small black boys in velveteen jackets, large lumpy garishly lipsticked hostesses, two Diamond Lil-style piano players, striped shirts, elbow garters, sideburns, monster steaks . . . In this restaurant I say I am thinking of changing jobs. I watch her intensely without letting this be felt. I've sworn to myself that I will not say one word less than the truth or more. I've said nothing untrue. I've said plainly and simply that going on without making some change is impossible, unfair to everyone, there'll have to be changes and beyond that I can't think. I leave a cloud of ambiguity. I have gotten only this far in my thoughts. I am lying but I don't know precisely the nature of the deceit. I say that I know I'll be leaving Boston—no other way to bring about a change. No place to go but New York. I am speaking elliptically and allusively, aware that I am putting a burden upon her, pleading with her to be tactful, careful, patient. It isn't my mode of speech. I seem to be learning a foreign tongue as I speak.

"You can't do it," Jean tells me. "I'm not going to—"

She breaks off and then says very simply: "Hope is a disease."

I press after her with my voice, aroused because she looks away. She looks sad and defeated. I tell her there's nothing new for me in thinking of change. Before, there was no reason, nothing but restlessness behind such thoughts. . . . But even then I wasn't fast-fixed, people knew this much about me. I feel angry and frustrated, I'm putting a case, I expect my words to be honored, I'm not a fool, can she possibly take me for a fool? People know I'm restless, I might at any time Break Out. I feel a lightness in my voice that's inhumane and spurious but I can't change it. I see her face smiling, I've never before seen her wan. In my guilt I mean to stop her at any cost from appearing in my eyes this way. I lean forward joshingly, telling her if we don't eat, the Klansmen in the room will blow up the car.

"It's not my luck," she says. She looks past me still in the candlelight. The pianos sound mechanical, unstoppable. A cigarish jowling voice is laughing, napkin at the red face. "I know it's not my luck, so I don't think about it. I just say, Girl— Oh hell, he's so strong and clear and drives me out of my mind, fantastic, people wouldn't believe me anyway if I showed him off, and he moves so well and he makes the words so different. 'My heart soars'—that happens. Everything ever said happens. He's so full of love he even loves— He has these cats and dogs, and it's not my luck and I could cry. I mean cry about the cats and dogs, he can't give them up, she said sympathetically, and I know and I *could* cry but you notice I'm not. I don't. Why bother? Sweetness, you mustn't ever talk to me about it, it's not fair, don't you see? Please?"

My hotel is full. We've flown in twelve hours early, a schedule change. I browbeat the desk, they make calls, find a room around the corner on Park Avenue. Jean comes with me and sits in the lobby while I register. We're exhausted, it's late at night. Neither of us realizes that we are waiting with the boy for the elevator directly in front of the night clerk with whom I registered as a single. Jean leaves me in the morning. When I come down to check out, the day clerk is breezy and the bill is high. At the top I read: "Gordon Flint and (1)." I write my check as the clerk goes on about the weather. Outside on the street I take my breath in deeply. "And one," my mind says aloud. For an instant I stand in the shadow of the clerk's knowingness, almost abashed. But at once I straighten myself, I recover. I see again "and (1)" and think: With these words, on this paper, in this phrase— Solemn, iron, I think in scorn of smallness, With these words I thee wed. The cave glints. I go on, head up, defiant, repeating inside me, And one, and one.

# 23

Here I am in the sun [my wife's letter said], wanting to say something and what can I say? Casey used to sit in her room listening to "One Man's Family" Sunday afternoon—I still hear the organ—and there were all these highly civilized voices being gentle with each other and facing their problems and facing each other. One was named Paul. I can even remember how some others sounded but I can't remember the names. I don't know why I'm thinking of this now. The point is I feel trapped, Gordon. Frustrated. I can't move or think. I sometimes almost see that it's hard for you and that you're going through something extremely difficult. But I can't bear to think that way. That's what I mean by being trapped. *I can't bear the idea of touching the wound.* That's why the "One Man's Family" business. They sat around talking out their problems and facing them or something and you could do that because it was the radio and none of it true or happening to the people.

And it wasn't bad to be middle class; it didn't all go without saying that we're awful. Not in those days. Well, I'm trapped in the middle-class silence. I see a hundred things. I see I should never have done what I did—make a life completely unthinkingly dependent on you, your interests, your wants and hopes. Of course not, it was ridiculous. I don't think that's bitter, just a fact. Everybody knows this now. It wasn't so clear when we started out, but I guess it was to some people. I was dull-witted. I thought, Children, family, love, hearth. . . . There wasn't any "etc." because I didn't feel superior to any of it. I wasn't "choosing between" things. I wanted nothing more. I also thought if you didn't have to have everything—95 Creative Activities and bags of money—then you would be allowed—Well, you couldn't lose what you did have. No doubt all of this is very historical and dependent on the Depression and knowing about people being hurt, especially the demanding ones. So I see that. And I see that I really do mean to make it as painful as I can. Not nice of me. I'm surprised in a way that I can be mean so easily. I mean I'm not being large-souled. I don't feel selfish when I say I want you to suffer. I don't really mean "I want you to"—I mean—I mean that you have to suffer, that's all. I think it's not right for it to hurt only me when it hurts so terribly. It wouldn't do either of us any good that way. There wouldn't be any learning in it. It wouldn't be *true*. Oh I don't know what I mean. . . . We've shared pain before, I've even shared yours now and then. And I see this won't do any good. Suppose you do suffer? What difference does it make? Suppose I could make you suffer so much that you stayed with us—what good would that do? It's all the same now. Going and staying are all the same. What we had—I won't go on about it, I just mean that it's over, ended, I don't deceive myself, we can never have it back. So you should go. I see all that—there's no purpose in "fighting for my man"—It's done, it's happened, it can't be brought back. But none of this— It's not what I'm trying to say. I've been dull and drab for so long. . . . I don't even know how to *try* to say it.

All right, it's like this, really: remember when you told us once at the table about the suicide center somewhere and somebody's doing research to see whether clichés are any test of the seriousness of the person who calls up saying he's going to jump? Does he speak in clichés? Well, here I am. I don't mean I'm suicidal. I mean I really do feel I'm walking the plank. The cliché's there, so then I'm serious. And that's what's so awful and useless about these words pouring out. They keep the reality from me. That's the real middle-class silence. That was what was going on in One Man's Family. All the talking at least fended off the reality. *I can't think of it. I can't bear thinking of it.* I don't let it come into my head even for a second, because when it does I turn to paper or something. I feel that I'm burned and ashes and if you even touched me I'd just crumble into nothing, pouf—nothing left. It's too much, Gordon. You must see that. I want you to know it. That is the way it feels. Whenever for one second I let myself feel you're away, there *is* "someone else," today, this minute, this hour you're— I know exactly what it would mean to go off the plank. No I mean to be *walking out,* to be coming to the end, the edge— And so all these words keep that away—I can't stand having it so close. If I could go on writing, if I could keep pushing it back, if I could stay in One Man's Family, if I could just move away from life, facts, reality, the thing that's coming, the end of my whole life—

I'll put this in with your other mail on your desk. Friendly, helpful letter. Do you remember how girls used to put faces at the end of sentences, happy, glum, smile or downturning. I'm going crazy. I just sat here thinking of that and I was actually proud of myself for never having done that in my life, can you imagine? You'll be downstairs reading this and I will be upstairs, not in our room. I'll be awake and I'll hear you and the pillow will be wet as usual and I'll be ashamed of myself as usual. But at least you will have opened it. You'll have touched it, there'll be some words between us. Gordon, I never wanted anything more than to be your wife and I'm still that and I can't stop.

—Terror— That's what it is. I can't bear it—suddenly seeing this complete emptiness

# 24

Freddie gave a farewell party after the last trip. His house was predictably campy. Everybody stayed outside on the tiny terrace—it had spaced wood flooring and whitestones. Before the women could go out they had to put on Japanese slippers. The party was elegant, Freddie and Bert were teasing Jean, there was music. . . . Mean, tight-eyed, I told myself Jean was "in her element," was she not? When it was over and I was gone, she would be back with them and would have suffered no loss. How far had she committed herself, after all? Who could answer? They treated her as before. She had lost nothing. I felt a fury rising in me. It could be an end for us! I talked to the cue-card girl and to Bert's wife and to Freddie's housemate. I walked about the place being shown objects. As Freddie handed Jean another martini I said directly to her: "I'm leaving in fifteen minutes by the clock. I've got to get the early plane." Jean didn't speak, only smiled. I wondered whether she was drunk. I felt a fearful hardness and sickness in my brain. In fifteen minutes I rose from where I was sitting. It was 8:30. Watching Jean's eyes behind me with my shoulders, I explained to Freddie that I had a plane to catch, I was leaving, sorry, awfully nice, enjoyed it so much, miss them all, we'll work together again. Of course, love to, I told Bert. Miss you all. I shook hands around the terrace, smiling, avoiding Jean's gaze. There was a stoniness and weightiness and recklessness in me, it was the murderer's recklessness. I started up the steps from the terrace to the living room, but the way was blocked. She was waiting there.

"What are you *do*ing? I don't—"

"I told you. I have to leave."

Her eyes were bright, fearful. There was bewilderment, a girlish fright in them.

"But— You didn't *say* anything."

I was about to say tauntingly to her, Be careful, don't you see? They're looking at you, now they're looking away. They'll all know now. They're listening and you don't want that, do you—?

I took her by the arm and we went into the living room. I stared down at her. I was confused by the coldness and deadness in me, I did not believe in myself.

"I told you, I'm taking the ten o'clock."

"I can't go *with* you?" Her voice rose high. "You're not

even saying good-bye, you're not telling me *anything*— Oh my God, sweetness, you can't, you don't mean that. You *don't.*"

Her eyes—a weird disbelieving humor in them, disbelief, search for the joke. Her eyes said: But you cannot be this person.

"Meet me," I said, desperately, senselessly. "I'll get a cab and come back. Start walking to Fifth."

I went away from her into the hall and took my bag and left. I didn't turn around. At the Fifth Avenue corner I waited for a time, watching shadows in the Grosvenor bar. Questions kept rushing at me and I shook them away like beggars. . . . Did she mean not to let me go? Did she think, was she . . .

Inside the cab I told the driver to go around the block and then east slowly on 10th Street, I was looking for someone, probably wouldn't appear, but anyway . . . I was on my way to the airport, somebody to share the trip.

"A woman," the driver said. "I get you."

In a moment I saw her. I opened the door.

Her face was still unbelieving. She stared at me. It was as though she had seen something she had not even been able to imagine. "You can't do that again," she said. "I couldn't live," she said. "I couldn't live the next minute."

I crushed her hands on my knees.

"Don't you remember? Don't you remember when I left the note? Oh, sweetness, this is worse, this is the worst thing. I don't have any insides. They're all gone, you took it all away. Tell me you didn't— You wouldn't have gone."

"She *knows*," I said. I meant to say: I'm a father. I wanted to say this. My children aren't cats and dogs I must have them I must have them something let me have something.

I held her against me and looked out at the streets and cars. I felt her trembling. I didn't know what I felt. She had told them something. She had come after me. She had said, Let them think what they want. She was mine? Nothing to us but trust? I held her against me strongly and worked my mind, searching myself, searching her. In the tangle of my brain there wasn't one true word.

# 25

On the plane people began screaming suddenly. The lady beside me was out of her mind. "Mother Mary," she screamed. There were thumpings in the air, arms that threw the plane down through air like a doll bouncing. Children were crying. No stewardesses. I saw somebody dart toward the shelf above seats in the front of the section, reaching for something. "It's falling apart, I feel it," the lady beside me said. "Isn't it? It's falling apart. . . . Oh Mother Mary, are we going down?" I held her hands and kept talking to her, and we fell through, off, fell off, downward sickening nothing-holding emptiness beneath us and a jolt. A creaking in the plane as though the metal were wood . . . The woman threw herself at me, the belt twisting her, "Mother Mother Mother," she was crying, her cheeks streaming, lavender scent thick. Holding her and talking to her I had a twinge of fear and imagined in one instant the crush of flame, eyes burning in my forehead, crazy toppling terror of going down—and then nothing. The fear vanished.

It was over in a half-minute. The woman didn't look up from my chest at once. The plane was full of children weeping, the pilot's voice returned, "Bumps . . . perfectly serviceable . . . sorry about that." The woman sat back. She turned and began praying, moving her lips, ignoring me. The stewardesses came by together speaking to each other. Looking out at the air I realized I felt regret. Faint but real. I thought back carefully to the beginning and saw I hadn't wanted it to end. Let me die, this had been my thought. I want to die. Nodding at my face in the window, I thought with a kind of sober appreciation: Nothing frightens me any longer, because I want to die. The more I thought this the stolider I grew, and the prouder.

# 26

A man who had worked in visuals and left came up from
the city looking for character references, someone to speak
for him in court. Herman Weinberg. He was a bystander,
he said on the telephone. He was standing on the curb in
Times Square, he had stopped to listen to a religious nut
preaching and the nut didn't have a permit or whatever and
the cops began leaning on him. Herm said, Wait a minute,
watch it with the brutality, the next minute he was in jail,
trouble, resisting arrest, hitting officers, profanity, obscenity
. . . the book. He needed a witness. He had gone everywhere but people were scared of him, who knows why.
They wouldn't even give him a bed. Listening, thinking at
once of seeing Jean, I remembered the face. Herm Wein-

berg, eyes squinting in some telephone booth against the smoke of his cigarette. He was grubby, I remembered. Overheated, overexcited. Hazy around the eyes, peering, starey. Drug-ridden? Cigarette packs in ruins, dirty, crumpled, flattened, splayed. I remembered Weinberg. Whenever he stopped talking and listened to you, he smiled and continued to smile. It didn't matter what you were saying. A crazy amiability. But no, he was not stupid. I could see Jean. I cut off his protestations with questions. Place, date, did he need money . . . I would be at the courthouse at 9:00 A.M. on the right day.

At supper after the boys left, I talked calmly about Weinberg's case, hearing with satisfaction a note of even-tempered protest in my voice. Of course the fellow was probably shot as a man, a professional, maybe a wreck. . . . He didn't say what he was doing. But wasn't it in exactly this sort of situation, I said, that people were supposed to rally around, carry a bowl of soup? His friends, people in the section his own age, people who had him to their houses and he and his wife had them back—presumably among those at least one person might have felt a sense of obligation. It made you feel, I said—as I spoke I felt no quiver of slyness—it made you feel as though people really were terribly dry inside, juiceless, incapable of caring any longer than they had to care. . . .

I sat waiting. I was certain that any moment my wife would say: *When are you seeing her?* Her voice would cut into the lie, open the skin, free us. The room grew tighter and firmer around me, and I went on, remembering or inventing a conversation I once had with the man, claiming that talk about people's dryness was the line Weinberg himself used to take about his co-workers when he came in to chat. I said that in those days I laughed at him and told him he was talking clichés, why didn't he open his eyes. I felt my wife's eyes move at the word *clichés,* move away and then cover the word as though I had traced it out before us in sand. I truly did not mean for her to keep silent, I was not trapping her in my deceit, I only meant to connect in her mind the justice of my going forth with general justice, I was excusing, apologizing. . . . A payment to conscience. It's right for you to go, my wife said finally. Our eyes didn't meet. "Somebody has to do it," she said. "It's not right for everybody to fail him. . . ." I interrupted her, shrugging off claims to virtue. But still I heard our voices lying on their tongues, saying not the words we spoke— "You wonder what people can possibly be thinking about. What do they think being human means?"—but others too accepting, blind, too wholly unbrave.

# 27

"Exhausted," Jean said. "Everybody's been blah-blah-blah-ing about next year and I'm so pooped I want to sleep the whole day. That's what I'm going to do. Oh sweetness, it's so nice. It's such a lovely surprise. I told them I was feeling terrible and I wasn't even going to answer the phone and I made a story for old Donna-love. I can just sleep and dream and lie awake about you and wait here like an expensive whore, I love you so much . . . I'm a ruin, I'm ruined, I don't have a life any more, I listen to that Schubert and . . . Leave me something, leave me your letters, I want to look at you while you're gone. I want to keep you here—"

I was distracted, confused. Her ease and cheerfulness—the poise that let her walk across the lobby and announce the floor to the elevator man, knock at my door and stand in the doorway and smile at me . . . In the hallway a maid passing. Jean came with a Bonwit's shopping bag that had a pretty robe in it and tiny slippers and a book of essays by Mary McCarthy. It should have set my mind at rest, should have made me less nervous, distraught—but no. The feeling of crowdedness, off-centeredness, errands undone . . . I saw myself turning this way and that, preparing faces, not touching ground. Trucks smashed the dawn air around me in my car beside the highway; I was talking hard on the telephone for no reason, Doctor Flint, often a guest, a room to nap in for the day. Not at all, fine, come right on in. Fine. Front. Doctor Flint is going to sleep in, tired out traveling. . . . And then the call to Jean and her coming . . . I was already late. The lawyer said 10:00 A.M. I had to rush. I hadn't even explained Weinberg's case, why I was there, what I was doing, when I could be back. . . . But Jean had made her stories, one for the office, one for "old Donna." And here she was—and I was leaving, and she hadn't asked questions. I'd "installed" her, told her I'd call, I'd let her know, I'd be back as soon as I could. I kissed her lightly and now—

The elevator man said Down. The car was empty. I said good morning brightly, wanting plainness, weather talk, winter ahead, sense of ordinariness. But the operator was silent. I stared at myself in the side mirror with no easing word, no commonplace, from the closing to the opening of the doors.

# 28

"All right," the lawyer said. "The client wants to defend himself, fine. I got to have forty dollars for advice, he can't do without advice. They won't let him, they'll legal aid him to death. I got your address for the rest."

"Who cares?" Weinberg said. "What's the difference, I'm done, I'm going to kill myself, why should I care?

"I'm not telling all I know," Weinberg said. "Forget it, I'm finished. I'm fucked up and I want to go back. I want the tit, that's all, I'm finished. I was born here, now I'm back, I'll go up to Riverside Park and slit my wrists in Riverside Park. That's it, that's it. But first I want that cop.

"You don't know what it's like," Weinberg said. "Forget it. I don't know my own home, my own city. . . . I said to the analyst, Listen, you know I even hate my own kid? He says, Herm, you fucking hypocrite. My own analyst, 'you fucking hypocrite.' This is what you want, hunh? You want to be the kid? You want to make them take care of you, hunh? Man, I'm fucked up is all. I can't get through.

"I've got the symptoms," Weinberg said. "Conversion symptoms. It's got a name. I got a band here like a chain, a regular chain across in my head. I haven't slept for four months, a half hour a night. But listen, you know me, you know the truth about me? I love my wife like a man loves his wife but I really do love my kid. I always knew it, I mean she's it, that's all, I love that kid. I'm going to take her away and make her into something gold. So what happens, Lily moves out. I go see her, I bring the kid to my room and it breaks your heart. Ellen. Nice places all the time. What does she know? She stands in the doorway and says to me, Daddy, you like it this way? Man, what is it? I'm fucked up, face it. You should never answer the phone.

"Hey," Weinberg said, "what is it at the Rexall? I used to eat lunch when I was in the building and they're crazy. I come back and it's eighty cents for a cheese and bacon. Listen, forget it and give me a hot dog.

"Man, I was in contact," Weinberg said. "I remember the summer was beautiful. I went out every day, I just wanted to smell the little sticky leaves, and I'd come in and hug Ellen and Lil, and oh honey how are you, isn't life wonderful, wonderful.

"It's all gone," Weinberg said. "I'm not in contact. I knew I was going to make it. I was getting it, you know? I had it in sight, all right, I was fourteen, and the old man left us, my mother, three years she took to die and every day saying, Hermie who'll take care of you, do you think, you little shit? I was in contact, grasping the elements. Ah what the hell, I've had it. I want to go back, I want the tit, period. I missed it, I never had it. I didn't say a word. Man, how do I know? I'm fucked up, don't you see? I don't know what I'm doing. They want the lawyer, I don't want any fucking lawyer. I'm going to put that cop on the stand and ask him one question. Just one question. Man, they can't lie, can they?

"Fuck," Weinberg said, hitting his forehead, "of course they can. Forget it. I want to see it, that's all. Just let me see that and then they can kill me, go ahead."

"Am I the law?" the lawyer said. "I told them I'm ready, that's all I can do. We got to wait. They're going to break for lunch. Okay, you have to go out, okay we'll get an afternoon call. If we get a call early, I'll say you had to leave on a business errand, the character witness. They'll give us an afternoon. I've got it, forget it—you go do your work and enjoy yourself. You want to help your friend, just don't *not* come back, right?"

# 29

I called from the lobby meaning to ask her to come down. I had decided this in the cab. Love must not be fitted into a schedule. We could have lunch, we could be civilized.

"Oh sweetness, I read the papers and all your briefcase and I never dreamed . . . You work so hard. I could hear you talking."

I saw her lying in bed, holding the telephone, waiting for my voice.

"I'm coming up."

"Sweetness, no, you're right. The other way is right. I'd be awful."

"You're telling me something."

"But don't you see—" Suddenly she was speaking very

fast and definitely. "You mustn't," she said. "You mustn't do that. You mustn't be nervous about me. We're going to have a nice lunch. We're not going to hurry. And then you can go back there and then you can come back here. We're going to have a nice lunch, and whatever we have together isn't going to be— We're going to be human. We're going to wait and wait like the slow movement. Dearest sweetness, we have to be human, it's all we can be, you'll wait for me, won't you wait, won't you please? And we'll have a lovely slow looking and longing lunch. We'll talk about music. I'm almost ready and you'll wait right there for me, won't you. You'll wait right there?"

# 30

I was late—Weinberg was waiting for me on the smelly
stairs, mad smile on his face. "Man, you bombed. Where
were you?" He began talking incoherently. There were two
cops. There was Dumbo that couldn't talk, all he knew was
bop and spit. And the other that came along and restrained
Dumbo. And Weinberg was handling his own case only so
that he could get at the dumb cop and show him up for the
*stupide* he was. And what happened! The dumb cop never
even appeared and the nice one lied like crazy! . . . The
lawyer came out of the courtroom beckoning furiously at
me. Come on, they're ready, waiting. I was sworn while
people walked about. I barely heard the questions. How
long had I known Weinberg, ever know him to be in any

trouble, responsible man? You never heard of any trouble, you'd say he had a good reputation among the people you knew? They were tired of their own questions, they couldn't think of anything to ask. When did you last talk to him? Saw him when? Before that, when did you last see him, when did he work for you, you last saw him regularly when he was still working, not lately? All right, go along. You came to prove something, we let you do it, we waited for you because we're on the same side—good people, above the dirt, stick by others once at least, give them one break.

Not guilty of resisting, the judge was saying, guilty on disorderly conduct, sentence suspended, don't let me see you here again, an educated man.

In the hall a policeman going by spoke over his shoulder to Weinberg.

"Hi, professor," he said. "Fuck you too."

On the street Weinberg told me he was selling his books, what good were they, he'd send me the money right away. Here I was, he said. Man, it was beautiful, there was even one person, enough to start a religion. Listen, he said, are you staying anywhere, I mean I'll give you my room, I got two pads, don't worry. When I said I had to go back, he turned, wet-eyed and wondering. You mean you came just for me . . . ? There were no cabs. The sun held no heat. Weinberg ran across the park, flagged one down. He was out of breath, dirty. "Man, I love you," he said. "You're a fucking hero. I love you." I shook his hand. Take care of yourself, forget the money, keep in touch. Weinberg shut the cab door sincerely. There were tears in his crazy eyes. I shook my head as we went off. "Lies lies lies," I said out loud, not caring who heard. I wanted everything to be over.

"You're so right," the driver said. After a minute I noticed I was in a gipsy cab, no photo, no shield. I shrugged and sat back and shut my eyes at the city.

# 31

In bed I was inside Jean, beginning to talk to her, and she pulled away from me. Her head was in the pillow. She was talking into the pillow. It was as though I had never seen her back before. Her shoulders trembled and heaved as she talked. I pulled the sheet over her shoulders gently, I tried to stroke her back. She was hysterical. "I just need fifteen minutes. It's a spiritual problem. It's just mechanical. I don't know what it is. Don't you see  . . .  There's no waste in it, don't you see? Don't you see—"

In a minute she began talking again. She was in tears, and her shoulders would not stop shaking. She told me everything was practical and sensible, it was too demanding. Suppose when Donna moved out and she had the whole apartment to herself and perhaps I could charter a plane for a few hours at noon maybe and we could fuck at lunch-time and not waste any time at all. I had never heard her say the word before, it whipped my mind. Her head was still deep into the pillow. I had a massive sense of helpless-ness, watching her shoulders shaking. I know you can't do anything, I know you can't stand it, can't stand it without the cats and dogs, that's all, isn't it? It's them, but no it's not, she said, it's nothing, nothing, and now she couldn't stop talking. Oh my God and this is all we have and I can't do it and it's mechanical. I'm whining. My God, I'm losing everything. I've tried so hard never to whine, not care. . . .

I touched her face with my fingers. Then I stood up and began dressing. I told her she was right, if we went on we would tear up everything we had had, we would ruin it all. She looked at me. The fear in her face was terrible. She told me she would lie endlessly, she would steal, hate, murder. There was nothing she would not do. She begged me to tell her I didn't want to go, there wasn't a hint in me of want-ing to go away from her. I touched her again and asked her to read my face.

We were like strangers of the same sex dressing together —a ward, a public room. Her eyes were red. There was a queer steadiness in me, a sunken weighted firmness. Jean's face tormented me, it looked scoured. Wept on for ages. We can have supper, can't we? I told her. I'll drive you home.

I called for the car, and when it came she went down

with me and went out and sat waiting for me while I paid the bill. She had never been in my own car before. She sat very straight, apart from me. I didn't speak. I drove uptown a few blocks and asked her where we should eat. She moved her shoulders and mouth and I knew she couldn't yet speak. I told her the stores were open, we could go to Bloomie's and buy a tie. We smiled at each other. We had done this together once. We parked the car and went to the store and bought a tie, grave with each other and the fairy salesman, and came again into the crowd, into the chill bright bustle of the store-night avenue, and we clung to each other, remembering the feeling that people's eyes were upon us, people couldn't help seeing happiness and beauty in us. We ate in a crowded Schrafft's, allowing ourselves only one drink, and then I drove her home. I double-parked in front of her house, and we stood together by the front door talking hurriedly and fearfully in the damp air. I told her she knew why we had to stop, we could kill the only thing we had. She nodded. I told her that if she didn't think about eating proper food and citrus fruit, better diet, I would be furious. I promised I would write again. I could write but she mustn't, I couldn't stand it. I told her it was so good that we had at least— Her face was a storm, and at that moment Donna and Teddie came out the door, bright and fresh, passing by quickly, waving. I screened Jean from their glance and waved back, as though laughing. I touched my lips to her cheek and moved away from her blindly. I drove uptown slowly, unbelievingly. For a hundred miles I kept my thoughts from her, away from what she would then be doing. Then at last I stopped and called her. No time had passed. I had no sense of minutes separating us. She knew we had done this together, I said, she did know that? We were trying to be kind to ourselves, decent to ourselves, protective? She told me yes, she knew, and I must be careful on the road. She would think of me all the way home, oh if she could guard us always. . . . She was lying in her room looking at the ceiling, that was all, that was all she would ever do. I came out again to the car feeling stronger, truer. I spoke in a strong voice to the gas-station attendant, paying him off. It was late and I began driving faster, a bit faster. Home by midnight at the latest was what I had said when I left.

# 32

In the morning on the late train I read the paper through comprehendingly, column after column. But then in my office I locked the door, pulled the shades, stood by my desk and wept. I was amazed at the flow of tears. I sat and began writing and the words rushed from me. I told her I had come to my office in fair enough control of myself and had been sobbing and weeping from the moment I locked the door behind me and saw the telephone on the desk. "I get up to look at myself in the pane of the window," I wrote truthfully. "I see I'm puffy, Jean, a small hairless animal face, silly-looking. Hanging on to the molding I gave a great grunt of a capsizing sob—then I remembered to pull the shade down. There are always people across the way.

Or upstairs. If the sound I made came to them, they'd send somebody down to find out the trouble. It must sound like someone dying." I told her I had to sit as I wrote in an unnatural position, holding my chin away so the tears wouldn't hop off onto the paper. I told her that the sight of those words before me—Hop off, Hop off—ruined me. "I write in an unnatural position," I said, "and touch the things on my desk with my eyes as though electrical shocks could come from the sight of anything—anything that was ever in touch with you or could be. I can't touch the file," I said. "Your picture is there. It's the same even with the newspaper, the *Times*. Even that can wreck me." I told her I had looked in the apartment-ad pages, running my eyes down through the numbers to her street and then swinging away, drained. "Jean Jean Jean," I wrote, "I knew and didn't know how desperate, how wretched I could be, how impossible— Oh my Jean dearest, I can lose myself for a minute or two at a time," I said, and explained that waking up one of the boys that morning had helped me for a minute or two. But how could I live on that. I told her I had tried a dozen ploys—that I knew when the phone rang from now on I would pick it up as though it were a prayer, speak hello as a prayer—that I could even bless the callers, the speakers, for giving me the one instant of hope—that I couldn't cut off, blot out, everything in my voice that was there only for her. "O my darling, I see I was never in love before. I didn't know what it was. I've got to take off my tie, I'm thinking in my perfectly asinine way, because it's new and these tears and this snot—that word because

132

what does a word matter—what help is there—the tears and all will stain it. I can never end this letter, it's supposed to be the last but then if it isn't ended, if there isn't any close, no signature stuck at the bottom, then it would be within bounds for it to be part of another letter, everything endless— How much more," I asked her, "how much more can you bear? I worked—I see now that telling you the simplest thing—when I worked, dictated, planned, what was coming, all that . . . Telling you the simplest thing gave me so much . . . Every word said, Jean, every pretense of ordinariness," I wrote, "is so mean a lie. There is nothing to me except love of you, there can never be more than that. I can see you," I wrote, "I can see you, your mouth and eyes and your hair slightly forward as you bend forward, so soft at the side of your cheek. I know how you would feel. Oh my Jesus Jean all my heart— I can't speak I despise this trying to write— Oh my darling it's past words, it's past words, Jean my dearest dearest—"

I wrote this letter on lined sheets of a yellow pad. I tore them off and saw that some words were blurred, the ink running from my tears. I shook my head at myself and typed the letter on fresh paper. Then I folded the fresh copy and the original carefully and put them in an envelope. I unlocked the top drawer of my desk and opened it. I read the letter through again and locked it in the drawer. Feeling better I left the place and went home.

# 33

They were slow with the music fills, and Bert was upset but
he had a budget closing and he wanted me to know he was
doing his best for us. . . . Jean called me at my office to
tell me this a week later. Legitimate business. Her voice
broke, and I said her name and then waited and told her I
was listening. I felt myself breathing with her, suspended.
When she began speaking again she was in full control.
"The mother" was taking her away. The mother thought
she looked awful and needed a rest and a change. She was
taking her to Brittany for a month, quaint inn, blah-blah.
The idea was to rest. They were leaving right away. They
would be gone a month, she wanted me to have the address
anyway. I told her I thought going away for a bit made
sense. When she asked if she could call when she came

back, I said of course, how could she ask. She would call the night she came in, she gave me the plane arrival hour. I could be in my office maybe. We told each other in steady voices that a period like this could be helpful, a chance to get things clear, find out what could be done. There was only one thing, Jean said, and she reminded me that we had said long ago we would never end, final good-bye, on the phone or in the mail and now this meant we had to see each other again, so we haven't and couldn't be parted yet. I owed her one more sight of me. She spoke as though she were a prisoner. I told her we mustn't say anything we were saying, we would soon have everything wrong. We went on talking about nothing, and at last she said, Good-bye for a month, I don't know how I'll stand it. I said it was exactly the same for me.

The next morning I stayed home reading magazines and drinking coffee on the sun porch with my wife. The leaf show had begun and the sun was brilliant. In the afternoon I called and arranged an appointment with a management consultant who had written me a year before about changing jobs, and the following week I spent a strange day in New York. I left early and went straight to my appointment from the plane, as though the city around me didn't exist. The management man was eccentric—he saw himself as a hero, embattled, beleaguered. He asked me to call him Conrad, and told me he was a business existentialist. His smile flickered before it went on like a fluorescent bulb and vanished swiftly. His voice was deep and sure. "I faced what you face," he said. "The world closes in. Everything you want, future, money, comfort, pleasure, fringes, capital appreciation, attractive associates, work I liked, capital appreciation, career I built myself. The whole bit. Didn't owe anybody a thing—"

Conrad struck his open hand with his fist and looked intently at me. One minute before, I had seen some humor in him.

"I'll tell you something. There's a touch of perversity in a man," he said. He was like a radio Birchite. "There's a strange queer thing, and it won't let you go the lazy-daisy way. It wouldn't let me do it. I said to myself, Conrad friend, don't die till you die. Live your life, don't be lived by it. I knew if I waited past forty-five I wouldn't do it, I wouldn't want the game, the risk of it—not the cheap craptable game but the real thing. Are you equal to it? I said. Well, brother, here I am."

We had lunch at a Park Avenue club with a group that included a fat man with an English accent who asked me the name of my broker and whether I knew Johnny Carson the television star. Afterward I went by myself to a movie about a husband-wife team of kidnappers. The husband at one point in the movie said: "We are mad," and I knew what he felt, exactly how far away from ordinariness he and his wife had traveled. At the airport, weather closed down the shuttle. Instead of eating, I sat at a bar thinking sadly about drinking martinis with Jean. It was nine o'clock when the field opened. I drove home slowly from Logan falling asleep, as it seemed, every other mile. I wasn't careful enough. A light turned orange on a car ahead of me, and instead of beating it through, the driver stopped short and I crashed his rear end.

# 34

It was a half-mile to my house from where the accident happened. The collision sent me straight up, a blow above the temple and at my nose on the windshield frame. The car motor was still running. I got out, my hand a mess of seemingly colorless thick sticky stuff from my face. The other driver was an elderly lady. She screamed when she saw me at her window. Nobody was on the road. The colors kept changing and changing. Talking was like lifting something too heavy. I said I'd drive myself home for medical help, she should follow or else I'd meet her at the police station. The car drove one-legged. My younger boy— out of bed as usual—burst into tears at the sight of me. My wife was calm. She made me lie down, worked over me carefully. She called our doctor, then another, then borrowed a car, drove me to the man's office, stood by me smiling, frowning as the stitches went in. At the police station afterward, still muzzy and sickish, I wrote out an account of the accident, as did the elderly lady. Then my wife drove me home. I kissed the boys on the landing as they stood staring in their pajamas at my bandaged self. The staircase spindles and carpet were sticky with blood, finger marks. There were drops of blood on the radiator. "It could have been terrible," my wife said. "The visor helped." I nodded. I wanted to explain the possibility that I had willed this accident. I wanted to explain that once on an airplane I hadn't been afraid to crash and that perhaps it was a desire speaking again in me—fatal will, etc. But I lay there, and we were duplicitous together. I talked teasingly about my nurse, her talent, my talented wife, and about how Conrad the business existentialist was a fool, and about how the money-world grew yearly sillier, emptier, more sentimental-superstitious-trivial. . . .

In the morning I wrote to Jean at the Brittany address. A paragraph only. I said that the day before at night I had driven into the rear end of another car that was waiting at a red light, that I hadn't been drinking, that nobody in that car was hurt, that I'd been alone, I'd been thinking, she knew of what, and that there was a chance of it happening again with children in the car and I must not risk this. I named my injuries and told her we had been right in the first place, right to end it and now I was ending it again, hopping off. . . . I asked her to help me, not to call, not to write, simply let it go. I told her, unconscious of the sanctimoniousness, that I might be better for others dead than alive but the same didn't follow for anybody I happened to run down, and at the end I asked her to remember as I would remember.

Three days later my office read me an artfully incoherent cable signed with Freddie's name, written in Freddie's traveloguing style but with phrases dropped into it as in a code. Concerned about condition . . . Not for immediate release . . . Original agreement . . .

After supper the night Jean's plane was due I called about arrival times and worked out the probable schedule in my mind. She would wait until she was home or else call my office from the terminal. She would then try here? If she was still with her mother, she would call from Kennedy. More privacy. Ten minutes for customs, etc. Or less. At nine-thirty I said I was tired, wanted a bath. I felt taut and fearful. I was lying in a hot tub fifteen minutes later when the telephone rang. My wife answered. I heard her get up from her chair in my study. After a few minutes I climbed out, stood naked and dripping, listening. No sound. Later when my wife came up, I said: Who was it on the phone? She stopped short. Then she remembered and shrugged. I looked away. "Nobody," she said. "I said hello and nobody answered. I finally just hung up."

# 35

For a while that fall, I remember, I turned into a reader. A lover of masterworks. On my way to the kitchen one night I picked Shakespeare off the shelf in my study and to my astonishment began reading with excitement. What was new to me, astonishing is right, was the infusion of recognition, the actuality of matters which, when I was a schoolboy, had no substance at all. Everywhere in the famous books you found bits of experience, reflections, observations, touching what you knew. They made life more comprehensible, made my own character and action more comprehensible. Love is an accident, for instance, this is what I had in my head at one moment. We make much of it and we see and feel our importance by means of it but the importance is spurious. Who does it matter to finally? We're affixed to this one or that one, Bottom to Titania, and, truthfully, how much does it matter? On the other hand I could experience my own unmanning in a story. I would travel to a provincial town with an urbane man from Moscow, simply for the sight of a woman slept with on a vacation at some watering place. I would be transformed, like the urbane man, into someone who believes night watchmen are radiated with fond protective feeling at the sight of me walking in the mists of the seaside with my beloved. I read continously for a month or more and I remember best that through it all I seemed highly valuable —to myself at least. It seemed to me that my own mind had never been more interesting or fresher than during this period when, for the first time in my life, I discovered a true meaning or use of art: that of confirmation.

Within weeks my memory of Jean's face and voice began to change. I realized this one afternoon on the train —some problem made us stop. Across the aisle the card-players were laughing, knocking pipes on a glass ashtray. Then it turned quiet in the car. Looking out at a trace of November snow flying about, I realized what I had just seen in my mind as I was thinking of her wasn't Jean at all, but her picture—she had given it to me in the middle of the summer, the one thing I possessed, a joke souvenir from some airlines terminal booth. It meant, of course, that even this quickly she was no longer moving freely in my memory.

I felt new relief at first. I wondered, tenderly, how the days now went for her. What was it truly like? A winter fly staggered over the dirty window glass and I sat watching it, thinking of my own bad days in the month just past. Black mornings, mindless afternoons, chess, squash, cold showers . . . For weeks I had to fight my memory almost minute by minute. . . . Walking up from the train at night I felt the ruddiness pasted on me like a smile in a polio poster, and when I met people on the way and started to speak, a weight inside choked me off in mid-sentence. I came up my own street, and some ordinary thing—the smell of wood smoke, vague and sweet, or a dog staring at me instead of barking—caught my mind crazily and nagged me with schoolboy questions. Am I this man? Am I really walking here? And instead of mocking myself when this happened, instead of leering at my own asininity, I stood fascinated. I stopped dead as though the cant and clichés in my head were precious sounds, as though it was proof of my character or mind that I could vanish from myself, pretend to watch myself, look on at myself, hesitate in front of myself, all the while knowing perfectly well, for Christ's sake, that the man on the porch, the fellow jiggling his senses there for the joy of it, saying, Is this me? was nobody else but me. . . .

Christmas day I sat reading the *Times* in the living room and came on an item about a woman of thirty, single, living on the West Side, found dead, good family, rather well off. A suicide, holiday suicide. I remembered Jean reporting a conversation with Donna. Donna had said, as comfort: Once *I* was ready for the Verrazanno, and Jean had answered, Now I'm ready. She had told me this once on the telephone. I looked out over the rubble of the room, wrappings piled halfway to the ceiling, boys at a board game, turkey richness in the air. . . . In my mind's eye I saw Jean in a Lexington Avenue market buying food. Items she wouldn't eat. Crackers. Fancy cheeses. I looked again at the newspaper story, read it over to myself slowly, sat morose. Then, with a start, I brightened. But of course— She wouldn't stay in the city over the holidays. She'd go out to St. Louis, she'd see the mother and the father. No doubt Rory would be back and there would be club dances and the like? I remembered, smiling to myself, her solemn endorsement of the hot-fudge sundaes served at the "country club." . . . Still smiling, released from guilt, I went out to the kitchen and was animated about carving the bird. . . .

Slowly the city changed for me. The first time I came, knowing Jean was there and that I would not see her, it was bad. Every object was an assault, I was head shy, my eyes squinted at the place. The sight of a phone booth in the terminal from which I had often called her—the sight gripped my stomach with fear. Every girl was a threat. Every face was aggressive. At the luggage counter I saw the black-and-green plaid of her luggage and turned away like a criminal. A crazy, excited, anticipatory fear . . .

But after a few times it was different. The city grew more mysterious, deep. I would go in her direction and look again in the galleries along Madison and Lexington in the Seventies and above. As though daring her to appear. I began going again to our hotel and to certain restaurants where we felt safe. Remembering her coming into the hotel with the shopping bag, her eyes cool, I would think: Here is the city, a thousand acids against marriage. At dusk, mounting a bus, I would see a girl Jean's age or younger about to get off, and I'd think: Only an hour and then you can't go comfortably, not alone, not after dark. And I'd watch the girl, half smiling, pleased with my knowledge of the truths and hardships of her freedom.

But I owed Jean money! It dawned on me only after months. Toward the end I had called her—because she insisted—collect, so that we could talk uninterruptedly. We spoke for an hour at a time. The matter of the expense never came to my mind—all at once I realized we must have run up a bill for hundreds. I had never thought of it. In New York by myself one night I called her and asked whether I could come see her. Her voice on the telephone was first eager, then puzzled. Of course, she said, when? Now, I said. I can be there in minutes. I dressed quickly, carefully. In the cab going up Madison Avenue the driver turned to look at me and said, "They got Malcolm X." I stared at my watch. The driver asked me to repeat the address, and it had completely left my mind. I recognized the house and shouted. I paid him and then, climbing out, wondered, as I had done many times before, whether she was looking out, looking down at me. I thought of the old air conditioner. I thought of her phonograph. I remembered her pictures. The doorman wasn't visible. I went up in the elevator, down the corridor— How much noise my shoes made! I rang, and she looked a second through the glass circle and opened the door. Hi, she said. It was a long sigh. She was languorous. She was wearing a double-breasted robe, knee-length, green. Behind her I saw she had been napping in her bedroom. I was just taking a nap, give me your coat. I said she was looking well. No, she told me, I've gotten fat, I don't care now— And I realized she was fuller in the face. I no longer knew, standing beside her, whether she was pretty, beautiful, piquant. . . . I looked and searched for an answer. We did not touch. I didn't speak. Let me take your coat. I said I remembered where to hang it. I joked about the closet—no better than before. I looked again and read her name on the Head skis. "For somebody who's had all these troubles," Jean said easily, lighting a cigarette, "you look—" She stopped and told me she was thinking abut a drink when I called. I went into the kitchen and got out the ice. We were not awkward. I remarked that as usual no citrus fruit in the refrigerator, and she moved about the kitchen with the odd weariness and uncaringness I remembered. I grew stiffer in withdrawal from her. In the living room we sat and talked. I grew nervous, my teeth almost chattered. I moved away from her, I walked about. "I won't ask anything of you, I haven't, I haven't been a bother," Jean told me. She chided me again, gently, about sending the letter to her. I asked about Teddie and Donna, who have you seen? Freddie comes in, Jean said. That was hard at first. He asked me how you were and finally I just held up my hand. That was a bad moment. Norton G. is around, and everybody wants him and he can't satisfy everybody and he's funny. I remembered that "Norton G." was one of the writers. Bert and Anne, Jean went on— they've been nice, they match me up with people. Young men. Jean rolled her eyes. God's gifts to nowhere. I asked about her father. Jean said she'd ended up telling him everything. She told him she'd been very foolish, had fallen in love with a married man, it just came out somehow at Thanksgiving, she couldn't help it. And they had another drink, and the father was terribly nice, he wanted so much to help. I was conscious of the smoke around her face, and of her knees. I wondered whether she had decided not to dress. When it was time to go I repeated again the ridiculousness of forgetting the phone bills, stupid not to— I could not put money in her hand, I moved toward a table, and she cried out suddenly, a distraught, fearful sound. No no don't. That's just terrible, don't you see— It's—

I told her of course, I never had any taste, crude, coarse. I was sorry. I told her we would see each other again. Perhaps the summer, I was going abroad. I want to touch you once, she said. She put her arms around my waist and held me briefly. I felt nothing. I had done what I came to do. Thank you so much for coming, she said. Jean, it's lovely to see you. And then I passed out the door, not thinking as I came into the night how I once stood and wept and wept. . . . Back in the hotel the phone rang. Jean told me it was so nice just to talk, just to see me. She thanked me again. I love to talk to you, I always will. I told her good night, and lay on the pillow for a time. Then I rose and turned up the sound on what I had been watching while we talked, and watched the late late flick.

In time I made accountings of her character, reviewed occasions when her behavior seemed poor. She was not above mocking people behind their backs. She was rather mean to Sylvie, the cue-card girl, highly condescending. When I once spoke to her about this, she was hard. She said, Oh she'd take old Syl out to lunch in New York someday and make it up. Then too she was harsh on the producer's illusions about his French and about his power to choose and pronounce wines. There was a definite streak of snobbishness in her. And the adeptness at deceit . . . Once or twice, before and immediately after Jean, I knew somebody passing through a period of domestic trouble—house breaking up and the like. I found myself staring at the new woman, noticing the way in which she was nervous, the way in which she was conscious of the gap of years, a wariness in her eyes and in the man's eyes. . . . I would tell myself that no matter how proper and decent and sane it might later be thought to have been, still there was the period of deceit beforehand, the period of lying, the time when the liars were within the deceit together, knowing each other as deceitful. I remembered times when I saw innocence peering straight out of Jean's eyes at Freddie or Bert when the very words that came forth from her were false. We had been liars together, and who could endure this and not be smutched?

* * *

Dozing one night in the rocker I heard voices. The boys were up? raising a storm? My wife was off at a meeting. I shook myself awake. My brandy glass sat on a pile of tapes. The bottom was warm. I touched it to my cheek. Cooler. The TV was on. "—thought it out, Tom," a girl speaking. "I've been nothing but a thinking machine for days and I learned something No let me finish I see it doesn't matter if you're never free *it doesn't matter at all* can you possibly understand my saying that?" I turned as to a gun. "I can't stop what I feel," the TV girl said. "It's so simple, darling— It's love and I'm too happy. I'm too marvelously wonderfully—" A man appeared in the frame. Strong-boned, older than the girl, eyes you cannot trust. "You can't just say a thing like that," he said. His voice rose. I saw the man sincerely felt terrible. "You've got to *think*." But the girl was in his arms. She kissed his throat, he began to speak and she was kissing his lips, murmuring in his mouth. The man pressed her into him. She was tall. I felt her weight in my arms, she was so slippery and living inside her clothes.

I stood up quickly. The cat looked at me from the couch and gave a neat yawn. The fire cracked against the screen. I turned off the lamp and the TV, and waited. The light pinched itself out in the glass.

I said Jean's name gently, the sound barely leaving my lips.

I sat down again and built up the TV faces in my mind and the words the actors had been saying to each other. Rocking a little I went over them like a boy checking a treasure box. A cedar scratched at the window. I peered forward. I said her name again but nothing came. Swearing out loud suddenly I gripped the rocker arms, and for a second the whole length of me was knotted. Then my eyes were hot and my face poured down authentic delicious rain.

# 36

That spring I was waiting one night in the TWA terminal for a London flight call when Frank, the lighting man, tapped me on the shoulder. He was jovial and full of gossip about people on the project. He ran through a dozen names, some of them I couldn't remember. We shook hands and were hearty, and I asked him to pass my good wishes on to anybody he saw—how we used to fight, etc., Kliegl, Bert, the others. "Marty I can't get through to," Frank said, his face turning automatic somber. "He went up in a plane with his kid and a friend and they crashed. It was the friend's plane. Marty Kliegl, he daid." We looked solemn together. I asked about the children, the wife, and then we were cheerful again and said good-bye.

The plane's main body of passengers was a group of training stewardesses. They hadn't been to London. I mentioned various places they'd like. . . . A tall Texas girl named Sally sat beside me and drank brandy from my flask, and the lights dimmed over the ocean, and very late I held her breasts and kissed her with my tongue in her mouth, and the following night we ate together and I stayed until morning in her room. On the flight back I sat in my seat watching the stewardesses pass back and forth, and kept hearing the Texas girl saying: "You know ah don't know what's come over me. They all know ah'm sittin' here tonguein'. When the super finds out, ah've had it. What am ah *do*in'?"

It was at about this time that I became more attentive to myself, thought about personal care, "grooming," etc., expensive smells and the like. A new tailor in New York did something for my unshapely ectomorphic self. Dressed for work in front of the closet mirror I saw a figure that was softer, easier, less tightly framed. I gained weight; my face filled slightly and felt smoother to my touch. People spoke to me curiously, asking me what I'd done to myself, I looked different, I looked "much better." I had a sense of myself as having moved on. I looked over my shoulder condescendingly at my former self.

I was better with them all, furthermore, less personal, less touchy with the boys. I didn't press them as hard, understood their failings as well as my own. I didn't turn bitchy, didn't hint by looks, etc. that I'd been deprived.

Look at me, look at this stinking "fidelity," tears, agony—none of that. As for the people roundabout—I lost my contempt. I saw the dry necks still, yes, souls exhausted in work, people vanishing into their upper lives. But I knew enough to think, Who's better, who's worse? We are what we are.

And when we had company—people coming in, neighbors, new people for coffee and brandy . . . When that happened, I knew everything that would be said before it was said. Sitting opposite them in front of the fireplace, one couple to a couch, thank you, looking over the coffee table at them, I'd know why the girl was enjoying my wife, and why I found a certain interest in the man. I'd know what my wife's opinions about them would be when they were gone and what they, this new young couple, would tell each other about us. And none of it hurt, that is the point—the foreknowledge, etc. There was a time when the idea of seeing my wife and myself this plainly would have bothered me. I hated an evening of predictable talk. Now I smiled, I was pleasant. Why wouldn't a person be interested in the facts about the company? It's almost unique. How we started, where we ended, exciting stuff in "the shop" just now . . . I even enjoyed seeing how careful people were with us! Watchful eyes so alert for a hint of a mistake, an off-putting or incorrect thing—they're flattering! I'm doing something: I think this to myself on these nights. I am helping a young couple. I am providing a vision of an established family, content, not uncreative, rooted, aware of hard moments in life but not defeated by them. Standing on the porch with my wife, seeing people off, light thrown into the blackness from the open door behind us, I wave attractively. They'll be all right, they'll manage. I hold the screen door for my wife. Nice pair. They'll be all right. Fare forward fare forward

—*Sweetness.* Always when I hear Jean's voice it says: *Sweetness.*

As I say, I go walking. Any night that seems long I walk for a bit, and though she's gone, I tell "us" over. Once or twice since then another girl, but this alone mattered, this alone. Jean. I tend to say her name as I walk. Afterward, whistling for the dog on the front porch I think: There was a time when my wife looked off with repose and happiness at a car going away from our house through the darkness, and turned back to our door with a weightless heart. I think: And that's all gone. Jean. I wait for a while, savoring the gravity of the losses. And that's all gone, all gone. Alone on the porch I whistle again and the moonlight flutters—the dog leaps the low hedge over his shadow and flounces up the walk. I let him in without speaking, impatient with frivolity, and stay outside in front of the pinging screen thinking until my mind—not slow at this, never slow—moves on in its kindness to something else.